DEDICATION

To all who strive, in addition to the veneration due to its origin and sacred name, to keep Christmas alive as a season of joy, giving, and love.

SPECIAL THANKS

To my wife, Gwen, my partner in life and in my writing. So many Christmases together, too many wonderful memories to cite.

THE JOURNEY HOME

(A Christmas Miracle)

Vincent J. Sachar

TABLE OF CONTENTS

CHAPTER ONE

Home for Christmas

[December 21]

From the window of the small commercial jet, she peered out over the landscape dominated by thick forests filled with pine trees. She was born and raised here, but for the past few years she had become far more familiar with asphalt, cement, and high-rise buildings. Snow draped the tops of the trees and carpeted the ground assuring that this would be yet another White Christmas.

The wheels of the plane touched the tarmac at Yellowstone Regional Airport in Cody, Wyoming with a bounce, followed by grinding screeches and moans before slowing down. The pilot redirected the craft towards the gate. It was at this point that most people would rejoice in the fact that the flight was over and someone was anxiously awaiting their arrival. But, Jody Newman sighed deeply. She was not "most people" and this was not where she originally intended to spend the holidays.

Jody's reactions were not indicative of any negative feelings towards her family. She certainly did love them. It's just that they were so... well... so... "backwards" was the descriptive word that came to mind.

꩜

Before her flight had landed, Jody recalled the conversation just the day before that led to her flight to Wyoming.

"It's only five days until Christmas," Roxanne said. "and you have no idea what you're going to do."

Roxanne Fowler was Jody's best friend. They were seated together in Manhattan at a small Italian restaurant off of Sixth Avenue, also known as Avenue of the Americas. The restaurant was loud with clanging dishes, people engaged in conversations, and the oft-opening front door as customers entered and left the establishment. But, the food was particularly good and the accompanying smells of tomato sauce, garlic, cheeses, meatballs, and a variety of spices added to the authenticity of this place.

Jody finished chewing her spaghetti, dabbed her face with a napkin, then responded.

"Well, Roxi, as we both know, I thought I was going to be in Vail skiing with Harold," Jody said, "until I found out he's involved with a girl in his office. I wasn't expecting to find myself breaking up just before Christmas with my boyfriend of nearly three years."

"I'm glad you found out what he's made of now," Roxanne said.

Jody took a slug of her ice tea before responding.

"Harold was always complaining that I didn't have enough time for him. He said my job was more important than him and our relationship."

"Well, like I've told you," Roxanne said, "I'm committed to being in Danbury with my family, but you're more than welcome to come with me."

"No," Jody said. "Thank you, but this is your time to spend with them, especially with your dad having recently come through major surgery."

Roxanne paused and took a bite of her food before making her next suggestion.

"Jody, it's been forever since you've seen your family. You barely saw them when you were away at college and have not been home since you moved here to New York more than three years ago. Why not spend Christmas with them? I know it's quite a hike out to Wyoming but spending the holidays alone thinking about Harold seems like a horrible idea to me."

Jody's mind raced along its own path. She stared down at her food and pushed it aside.

Well, no matter where I am, I won't be spending my time thinking about Harold.

Jody lifted her head and gestured with her fork as she spoke to Roxanne.

"Let me tell you, Roxi, I love my family. But going back there is like going back in time. I worked hard in my studies to escape that place and go somewhere that offers opportunity for success and advancement. If you live in a cabin on a small ranch in East Yellowstone Valley, nothing around you will ever change and you're going absolutely nowhere in life."

Jody looked up from her plate and stared at Roxanne.

"No, I think I'll take a pass on Wyoming. They're not expecting me anyway and I already sent gifts for everyone. Believe me, I'll be just fine here."

∽

Leggy at five feet seven with dark brunette hair, pouty lips, and high cheekbones, Jody turned heads wherever she was. Her skin tone gave a hint that she had Native American ancestry somewhere in her family line. Jody's eyes were large, oval shaped, and she was among the two percent of the world's population with green eyes. Hers had to be up there among the prettiest of them all.

Jody was athletic. She played on her high school basketball and volleyball teams. She was intelligent, graduating as the valedictorian of her class. She was an achiever. She gained admittance to college on a four-year scholarship and quickly, following her graduation, she was establishing herself in her new career in New York City.

Even Jody was surprised that it had been more than three years since she last saw her family. They came to her graduation from Oregon State University where she majored in Apparel Design and minored in Merchandising Management. Jody responded to an invite for an interview in New York City and was flown there. She was hired and was now working for *Fashion Imaginations, Inc.* (FIMA), a start-up sportswear corporation with an eye towards competing with the best in the industry.

Now, with only four days before Christmas, Jody would be spending Christmas in Wyoming. This would be the first time in several years that she celebrated Christmas at all.

It was a phone call from Jody's mom that changed everything. She called Jody just to tell her she loved her and wanted her to have a great Christmas in Colorado. Without any warning at all, the words just poured out of Jody, as if they had a mind of their own and didn't need Jody's approval to say what they did.

"Mama, my plans have just changed. I'm not going to Colorado. In fact, I was thinking about coming to be with you all for Christmas—that is, if you've got room for me."

Her mom's squeal of delight brought tears to Jody's eyes, though she worked hard to maintain her composure and not end up sobbing over the phone. Afterwards, Jody struggled with what she had done and regretted that she had opened the door to flying to Wyoming for the holidays. But, it was too late now. There was no way she could back out without hurting her mother.

As the plane reached its gate, Jody spotted her family peering out from a window. Her dad, Forrest Newman, was a burly man at five feet nine inches with a warm engaging smile. As always, he had a cowboy hat atop his head and wore a brown leather jacket. Her mom, Jolene, was a petite woman at five feet three. She wore her black hair in a bun. She was a pretty lady with dimples that highlighted her face when she smiled—which was pretty much all of the time.

Jody's sister, Misty, at sixteen, was maturing into the pretty young lady that she had always been expected to be. She stood at five feet five inches with curly brown hair that extended past her shoulders, olive skin, and hazel brown eyes. The twins, Rusty and Rylie, a surprise when they came along, but much-loved by Forrest and Jolene and everyone else, had just turned five. Rusty's blonde hair was curly and long. Rylie wore her blonde hair in pigtails. Other than hearing Jody's voice over the phone a few times, they didn't really know her at all.

Nick, her brother, was at work, but would catch up with Jody later in the day. He just celebrated his twenty-third birthday; three years shy of Jody. At six feet two, sandy brown hair, neatly trimmed facial hair and his mother's dimples when he smiled, Nick looked the part of a handsome young cowboy. After graduating high school, Nick stayed in the area working on one of the local dude ranches. Jody's Mom believed that Nick was about to get engaged to Lana, his high school sweetheart, but they had not, as yet, made an announcement.

Forrest Newman made his money by raising and breaking horses that he sold to the local dude ranches. He also raised beef cattle, sold some crops to local markets, and worked part-time on the same dude ranch where Nick was working. Forrest's income was limited, but more than adequate for his family expenses. There was no doubt that he loved the work he did.

"Having more money while forced to raise my family in places nowhere near as healthy and beautiful as where we now live, don't make a whole lot of sense to me," Forrest once told Jody. "There ain't nothing wrong with using your God-given talents to succeed in life, Jody, but there's a good many things that can't be measured in value by the almighty dollar."

East Yellowstone Valley lies between the Absaroka Range of the Rocky Mountains in northwestern Wyoming between Cody and Yellowstone. It serves as a gateway to Yellowstone and Grand Teton National Parks and extends through the Shoshone National Forest. It is a secluded western mountain valley where the plains and the mountains meet. Carved out of the thick forests are dude and private ranches. The Newman family ranch consisted of some 450 acres that had been in the Newman family for several generations. It was situated between Cody and Powell. The land, surrounded by a deep stretch of forestland, contained their cabin, a barn, a storage shed, a corral in which to work with horses, pastures, and some acreage dedicated to growing crops. East Yellowstone Valley was also home to the bald eagle, elk, grizzly bear, moose, mule deer, and big horn sheep.

Oh well, primitive, boring, a reminder of the lifestyle I escaped from, but at least I'll be making an obligatory family visit. Who knows? Maybe some downtime in an area where there's not much else to do will be good for me. No Broadway plays, holiday shows, no major department stores to shop in, zero local diners to enjoy a latte, and no theaters to catch a show.

Okay, so maybe I'm exaggerating a bit. Cody and Powell are cities and do have things there, but it's still going to be a radical change for me.

"Anyway, for the most part, guess I'll just sit around and listen to the pine trees occasionally drop some snow from their branches," Jody mumbled to herself and chuckled.

CHAPTER TWO

Deck the Halls

[*December 21*]

Christmas music was playing throughout the airport. Holiday decorations, colored lights, decorated trees, Christmas balls, elves, images of Santa were everywhere. Following the hugs, kisses, embraces, and smiles, Jody, her Mom, Misty, and the twins gathered luggage, left the airport terminal, and waited for Forrest to bring the SUV to where they were all standing. It had been cold in New York. It was beyond cold here in Wyoming.

"I'd forgotten how frigid it gets here," Jody said to her mom.

"Not to worry," Jolene said, as she opened her winter coat and shared it with her daughter. "We'll have the wood burning stove stoked up high and a fire roaring in the fireplace. In no time at all, you'll be toasty warm."

Sure, and smoke from burning wood consists of a mixture of gases and fine particles that can get into your eyes and respiratory system and cause burning eyes, runny noses, and illnesses like bronchitis. Plus, wood smoke contains several toxic harmful air pollutants. Guess I should have brought a protective mask and an oxygen tank.

Jody was surprised that both of the twins wanted to sit on her lap during the trip to the cabin and Misty talked non-stop to her big sis. In a sense, Jody was far removed from this place. To her family, she was not. In all the time that Jody had been away, her family never lost sight of her and the fact that she was still a part of them.

They arrived at the cabin and Jody's mouth fell open.

"Whoa, you've made some major changes here."

Her dad and mom both laughed aloud along with Misty.

"Yeah, I made a few changes," Forrest said.

"A few?" Jolene responded. "As you can see, he extended the porch at the front of the cabin and wrapped it around the back. He replaced all the windows with double-pane weather-proof glass. Those are new treated cedar wood shingles on the roof. And, when you get inside, you'll see we have a new master bedroom with its own bath and fireplace towards the rear of the cabin and a new second bedroom in the loft. That means we now have four bedrooms. Misty and the twins have rooms up in the loft. Nick generally stays at the dude ranch where he works, so our old master bedroom is available," she said with a wink.

"I also reconditioned and resealed the exterior logs of the cabin to match the logs that were part of the additions to the structure," her dad said.

"This is incredible," Jody said.

"Aw, it wasn't all that difficult, and I had help from Nick and a few neighbors. Besides," Forrest said with a smile as he turned to face his wife, "I loved doing this for your mom. The way I see it, she has always turned this place into a home in her own special and unique way."

Forrest leaned over and planted a kiss on Jolene's cheek. He then hopped out of the vehicle, grabbed Jody's luggage, and ran inside to stoke up the wood burning stove and start a fire in the large gray stone fireplace in the main living area.

Holiday lights were strewn across the eaves of the cabin and along the front porch. The sun was settling in for the night and the lights had turned on.

As Jody stepped inside, her mind was racing.

Are you kidding me? This place is awesome. Hah, and I'm paying $2,800 a month before utilities for my New York City studio apartment that's 450 square feet. It has little or no water pressure most of the time, hot water is a hit or miss, and the walls are paper thin. And this kind of construction for the add-ons in New York would be prohibitively expensive and would require a ton of permits and inspections.

Jody stepped into the main area of the cabin which comprised the living room, dining area, and kitchen. She glanced up at the exposed-rafter cathedral ceiling and also spotted the loft which contained two of the four bedrooms. She noted that her dad had replaced the black cast-iron Franklin stove with a larger one that obviously generated even more heat. The floor-to-ceiling gray-stone fireplace already contained a blazing fire. Jody's eyes explored the furnishings throughout the cabin. A leather couch faced the fireplace with an armchair on each side. To the right of the fireplace, she spotted the piano that her mother played. On the opposite side, Jody spotted a tall Christmas tree standing in a corner of the room near the windows that exposed the property at the back of the cabin. They had not yet decorated the tree.

"We left the tree undecorated until you were here with us," her mom said. "Nick is going to pick up Lana after work and they'll be here this evening. We can all decorate the tree together. I've got some fresh cookies that Misty and Lana helped me bake. We'll pop some popcorn, make some hot chocolate, and trim the tree together just like we used to do."

Jody noted the smile that covered her mom's face. She considered how such simple things could bring so much joy to her mom.

Decorate a live Christmas tree? For the last few years, Jody didn't even have a tree. In fact, she did not have a single Christmas decoration anywhere within her apartment.

The last tree I had was back in my sophomore year of college. It was a three-foot-tall silver artificial tree with red lights and red Christmas balls. It looked like something you'd see in the women's jewelry section in an upscale department store.

Mom's acting as if decorating a tree together is some kind of family holiday ritual that's supposed to mean something special. Like maybe the Christmas fairies would give us some bonus points for doing that. Truth is, I'd just as soon be tucked away somewhere going over some proposed fashion designs we hope to launch by the end of the first quarter of next year.

"Are you gonna help make the tree all pretty and shiny?" Rylie said, interrupting Jody's thoughts.

Rusty moved in front of his sister, with his little chest puffed out.

"I wanna help. I wanna help make the tree look good," he said. "I helped pick it out, ya know?"

"I did, too," Rylie said, while positioning herself back in front of Rusty with her hands on her hips.

Jody chuckled.

"Is that true, Rusty? Did Rylie help pick out the tree?"

"Yeah, we both picked it out. We did it yesterday, but mama said we gotta wait 'til you come, so we could descrate it together."

"Yeah," Rylie chimed in. "Mama said you an expert decrater person and you can help make our tree the bestest ever."

Rusty and Rylie were both staring up at Jody, nodding their little heads. Wide grins covered their faces. Their eyes sparkled and gleamed.

Jody laughed again, bent down, and pulled the twins close to her. She kissed each of them on the forehead.

"Okay, it's a deal. We'll decorate the tree together with all of us helping, but you two have to be special helpers, like Santa's elves, okay?"

The twins started to jump up and down and clap their hands. Jody considered just how pure and innocent these little ones were.

Wow, I can't believe how much I love these two little angels. How could I have missed years watching them grow—starting to crawl, stand, and walk, hearing their first words? They're so precious. What in the world was I thinking?

Once again, Jody kissed her little brother and sister and considered, just as with her mom, how simple things seemed to bring so much joy to them.

Rusty and Rylie ran off somewhere to play. Misty was now standing next to Jody.

"I guess you've seen the tree at Rockefeller Center," Misty said. "They say it's beautiful every year."

"Yes," Jody said. "It's one of those traditions that you just have to go see every Christmas Season. There's so much to see and do at Christmas in New York. The City comes alive, people seem happier and friendlier, acting as if Christmas really... "

Jody was about to say "mattered" but held back. There was no need for Misty to be negatively influenced by a cynical older sister.

In no time at all, the cabin was toasty warm. After giving Jody a tour of the new additions constructed by Forrest, Jolene sat with her daughter at the kitchen table. She made each of them a cup of hot tea and gathered up a few of the freshly-baked cookies.

"I still can't get over the fact that we have you here with us for Christmas, my love," Jolene said. "So, tell me all about how you're doing—at your job, living in such a big city, your relationship with Harold."

And before Jody could even answer, her mom leaned over and kissed her on the cheek.

"I'm so happy that you are here, darling. Having you with us helps make this a perfect Christmas."

A lone figure, dressed in dark clothes, wandered alone in the forest closer than ever before to the cabin where Forrest Newman and his family lived. The Newmans had never encountered the man. They were familiar with the rumors about the "the man in the woods"—a mysterious stranger said to wander about in the darkness of night. The stories expanded becoming more mysterious as time passed. To others, it was nothing more than mountain folklore—a scary story to share at night around a campfire.

The wind was beginning to assert itself with periodic howls and roars. There was a storm brewing and headed this way. Seems no one ever knew for sure just when a winter storm would arrive and how fierce it would be.

The man lifted his head and stared out into the darkness. He was sure something would be moving in within the next day or so. His movements were silent. His appearance was ghostlike—much like a shadow passing through the blackness of the night. Then, in the blink of an eye, he was gone.

CHAPTER THREE

When What to My Wondering Eyes Should Appear

[December 21]

They were getting ready to gather near the Christmas tree when Jody's phone signaled that a text had arrived. She glanced quickly and was surprised to see that it was from Alfred Monmouth, the CEO of FIMA.

Jody: Congratulations. New potential client from Japan, SAIKO Industries, interested in your apparel line. Need you here on the morning of December 25 at 8:30 a.m. for a meeting with them, as they will be returning to Japan on that afternoon. Please confirm.
—AdMon

Jody's hands were shaking, as she sucked in a breath of fresh air. This was the moment she was living for. A potential client had seen samples of prospective apparel that FIMA had to offer and had chosen the line created by Jody. She would share in royalties with her company, but the revenue she would derive would be more than she had ever made to date. And, if the deal went through, her name would be known worldwide. Jody bent over to take a deep breath and help control her emotions. She could hardly believe this was happening. This was incredib... uh... December 25?

She would have to be back in New York on Christmas morning. She would have to fly out sometime on Christmas Eve day. December 25? Really? Who does business on Christmas Day? How does she explain this to her family? Her knees started to bend then straighten. She sat down in a chair, blowing her cheeks out then either swallowing the air or releasing it.

Surely, my family will understand. This is my livelihood, my future. Opportunities like this don't just happen every day. In fact, for most people they never happen. And, there's more than me at stake here. If this deal falls through because I don't show up, FIMA stands to lose a great deal of money. And, I'll likely lose my job.

Jody could not shake the sick feeling in her stomach. She sighed, took in another deep breath, and decided she would wait before telling her family that she would be heading back to New York earlier than anticipated.

Rusty and Rylie came bounding into Jody's bedroom.

"We're ready, we're ready," Rylie said, as she hopped up and down and reached for Jody's hand to lead her to the tree.

"Yeah," Rusty said. "Mama made hot chocolate and it got marshmallows in it."

"Yeah, and we gots cookies and popcorn," Rylie said. "C'mon let's go."

And there was so much more. The Newman family was rich in traditions, some of which they adopted over the years from neighbors. Jolene made a chocolate yule log known as a *bûche de Noël*, a popular Christmas dessert or pudding eaten in France and Belgium where they are known as *kerstronk*. The yule log consisted of a chocolate sponge roll layered with cream and covered with chocolate to look like a bark-covered log.

"Ed Sylvester's wife, Monique, was born in France and learned the recipe from her mom," Jolene told Jody. "I got the recipe from her."

Red poinsettias strategically placed throughout the room added to the festive feel. Holly and ivy were sprinkled here and there. Candy canes, walnuts, peanuts, and pecans were placed in small bowls scattered around the room. Chestnuts tossed onto the fire in the fireplace crackled and split, indicating when they were ready to be eaten.

Jolene started the Christmas traditions at the beginning of the month of December. She participated in a cookie exchange. She asked Misty to help the twins write letters to soldiers, which Misty did also. She had the twins help mark down a Nativity Calendar leading up to Christmas Day. Jolene also taught the twins how to set up the Nativity scene placed atop a buffet in the room.

Jody stood near the tree with Rusty and Rylie draped all over her. Nick and Lana arrived and exchanged big hugs in greeting Jody. Lana, at five feet five, jet black hair, and a smile that could light up a room, was dressed in jeans, boots, and a western shirt. She certainly looked the part of a pretty cowgirl.

Jody imagined that you could almost hear a trumpet sound when her dad started the grandest ritual of all by climbing a ladder and beginning to string the lights on the tree. In order to better see the placement of the bulbs, Forrest had them all lighted as he wove them through the branches. Jody laughed as the twins oohed and awed and little Rusty clapped his hands. Jody reappraised her opinion about the value of tree decorating when she stared at the children. They were wide-eyed with broad smiles on their faces, standing transfixed as they observed the beginnings of a tree being transformed.

Wow! Guess I hadn't figured on how special it is to see the reactions of the children. They're responding to something pretty, something of beauty, a tree that stands for something positive. Far too often, what the world will offer them is dark, dismal, and negative. It is kind of nice to see how colorful lights shining through green tree branches makes them happy. No doubt that Christmas has a kind of beauty unique to itself, like no other holiday. Feels good to make others joyful.

Nick lifted Rusty, Jody lifted up Rylie, and the twins placed the first ornaments on the tree. The other family members all applauded as the two youngest giggled and bore a look on their faces as if they had just completed a monumental task. Jody marveled at how something so simple could generate so much joy.

Everyone took part in decorating the tree. They drank hot chocolate, ate cookies, popcorn, and roasted chestnuts. Jody's dad took the lead in singing Christmas carols and songs as they all joined in. They convinced Misty to get her guitar and play along with the singing. Jody also noted that Misty had a particularly pretty singing voice.

At one point during the decorating, Nick put his arm around Jody, hugged her, and kissed her cheek. He whispered in her ear.

"I'm so glad you decided to come and be with us this year, Sis. Having you here makes things even more special."

Lana was standing nearby and reached over and squeezed Jody's hand.

A wave of guilt surged through Jody's body and mind. She had come as a last resort when her boyfriend dumped her and she had no place else to go. And after she made the choice to come, she had doubts and regrets over her decision to do so. And now, she was planning to leave sometime on Christmas Eve day.

The temperature outside was dropping and another winter storm was headed their way. But, no matter how cold it was outside, it was warm and cozy inside the cabin—and a great deal of that warmth had nothing to do with wood burning stoves and logs blazing in a fireplace.

Once the tree was decorated, Forrest turned the lights off in the cabin until the only light came from the Christmas tree and the flames licking the wood in the tall stone fireplace. Lana helped Jolene make sure everyone was replenished with cups of hot tea, coffee, or hot chocolate. Some sat on the couch that faced the fireplace. Others pulled chairs in forming a half-circle. Rusty was sitting on Lana's lap. Rylie was snuggled up with Jody. Forrest was seated on the fireplace hearth with Jolene seated next to him.

In a moment of time, Jody was drawn back into her yesteryears. She remembered when her dad took out the same little book that was in his hands now and took turns with her mom reading aloud. She recalled how the words seemed to float gently in the air until they completed their journey and found a home somewhere in her heart.

Jody wondered what had happened over the years to quash the magic of moments such as these. What caused her to reject anything that was not measurable by profitability, professionalism, and stark reality? There was no room in her heart for nostalgia or things that only existed in worlds of fancy and the imagination. How did that happen? When did it occur?

"Twas the night before Christmas, when all thro' the house not a creature was stirring, not even a mouse," Forrest began.

"The stockings were hung by the chimney with care, in hopes that St. Nicholas soon would be there," Jolene continued.

As her dad and mom interchangeably read from Clement Clarke Moore's immortal poem, *A Visit from St. Nicholas,* Jody sat transfixed somewhere between what was occuring now and what had been rooted in her past. She remembered past Christmases when her dad and mom read to her, Nick, and Misty. She recalled that stirring within her as she pictured in her mind all that her parents were reading aloud to them. Hah, Santa, elves, reindeer, and the magic of Christmas itself were all once so special to her. She had believed in a child born in a manger within an animal shelter, whose birth was a purported gift to mankind.

When the reading was over, Rusty broke the silence by clapping his little hands together. Everyone joined in and laughed aloud as they did. Once again, Jody marveled at such joy emanating from a simple thing.

"I'm gonna stay up all night on Christmas Eve so's I can see Santa and the reindeer," Rusty exclaimed.

"Whoa, hold on, Rustoleum," Nick said as he reached over and tousled his little brother's hair. "No can do, my little man. If Santa knows you're awake, he'll just move on to another house and come back much later when you're finally asleep. They say one little boy stayed awake so long,

Santa almost went back to the North Pole without leaving the presents."

Both Rusty and Rylie were frozen and rigid, with their little mouths wide open and their eyes bulging. There was no doubt they would both be in bed early on Christmas Eve.

Misty was next as she took her guitar and sang a medley of Christmas songs. Jody considered that her younger sister was talented enough to make it in the music industry. As she sat contemplating that thought, it struck Jody that she valued everything in terms of whether it could generate money and fame. Of everyone in the room, Jody made the most money and was already in position to rapidly climb the ladder of success within her industry. She was the one living in the nation's most populated city. She was the one who attended penthouse parties that included top fashion designers and celebrities. She had already attended luncheons and dinners in restaurants priced well-above the budgets of the average person to eat dishes with names most people could not pronounce. She was the one whose fashion designs were already drawing the attention of people of considerable influence in the fashion industry. Jody could sit comfortably and have discussions with people of high intelligence and worldwide experience and knowledge.

Yet, as she glanced around the room at the faces of her dad, mom, Nick, Lana, Misty, and even Rusty and Rylie, she sensed a peace and a joy within them that could not be acquired from money or fame. Her dad and mom were happy and secure in their marriage. Nick and Lana appeared to be very much in love and focused on a future together. Jody could not even step away from her job and spend Christmas Day with her family. Harold, whom she considered she could possibly marry one day, was in Vail, Colorado with another woman.

Perhaps, Jody needed to reconsider the meaning of the word success.

∽

After such a full day, Jody was looking forward to a good night's sleep. She sat on the bed and replied to Alfred Monmouth's text.

Received your text. Excited at the news. I will be at the office on the 25th in time for an 8:30 a.m. meeting. Best, Jody.

She worked hard to put the New York meeting out of her mind. It was the least she could do to focus on her family for the limited time that she would be with them.

As she was lying in bed, she was surprised at what she was hearing—or not hearing. The sounds of traffic passing on the streets below her apartment, horns beeping, buses moaning and grunting as they stopped and started were all missing. The silence she encountered was deafening. And, there were no lights that she had to fight to block out from her bedroom windows.

She laid her head on the pillow and relived some of the day's activities—bringing a Christmas tree to life, singing with her family, feeling the warmth of their smiles and their love.

A smile crossed her lips as her head sunk deeply in her pillow. And then she drifted off into a peaceful sleep.

CHAPTER FOUR

Just Like the Ones We Used to Know

[December 22]

The sun had not yet risen when Jody awoke. Her eyes opened to a soft silvery glow as the moon cast its light on the snow throughout the area and generated a mystical feel. She kept her head snuggled on the pillow as her mind reflected back on the Christmases of her past.

She could not remember just how old she was when she saw the first family Christmas tree standing in the very corner where it was now in their cabin. She only knew that as she stood at its base looking up, it was incredibly tall. To a little girl, it had to be, perhaps, sixty, eighty, one hundred feet? The array and blend of colors, glitter, and shiny objects mesmerized her. She recalled her daddy lifting her up so she could place the angel at the very top of the tree. But, she couldn't quite do it herself, so he held her with one arm and helped her fasten it to the top.

"Daddy, how will Santa Claus come down our chimney when there's a fire in the fireplace? Won't he get burned?"

Jody was only five-years-old, the same age as Rusty and Rylie are now, when she asked her daddy that important question. There was no smile on her face at the time. She was worried—deeply troubled. Her anxiety was relieved, as usual, by the wisdom of her daddy.

"Ah, don't you waste another second worrying about something like that, little angel cake. Santa is magical. We honestly don't know how he does so many wonderful things. They're all just part of the reasons why he's Santa, you know?"

And Jody never worried again about the fire burning in the fireplace on Christmas Eve. In fact, on that very night, as she was lying in her bed in the cabin loft, she awoke during the night and was sure she heard something up on the roof. It sounded like hoofs, reindeer hoofs, pawing on the rooftop. Jody's little heart was bursting with excitement. She remembered being so overwhelmed with joy, she was paralyzed as she was lying there in her bed. She remained right there with her little heart beating fast and a huge smile on her face.

She was quite sure that, in a relatively short period of time later, she heard the sleigh fly away. She pictured eight reindeer towing a sleigh with Santa and his cargo traveling through the night sky until every present was delivered and they all returned to their magical home at the North Pole.

The further they moved into the month of December, the more the cabin would be decorated, the more Jody's mom would be humming Christmas songs and carols, and the more everyone's heart seemed to lighten.

When Jody was seven, she awoke Christmas morning to find a saddle under the tree and a note telling her to look outside. When she did, she saw a palomino horse. It had a red bow fastened to the top of its head. Jody squealed with delight, named her horse *Belle*, and, until she left for college, rode her several times a week.

At the age of nine, Jody awoke on Christmas morning and spotted a tiny stocking hanging at the fireplace next to hers and Nick's. That was when she first learned that, in a few months, she and Nick would have a new baby sister.

Every Christmas season, the cabin carried the smell of delicious baked goods, along with coffee, tea, hot chocolate, and wassail. Her mom also made homemade candies and a Christmas fudge. There was always a generous supply of oranges, apples, pecans, peanuts, walnuts, and hickory nuts, which were placed openly around the primary cabin room. When Jody was younger, she delighted in helping her mom decorate the house. Her mom placed ribbons, pine and fir tree branches, and hand-dyed braided ropes throughout the cabin. And, even back then, Jody had a keen eye for decorating. She'd walk over towards a display of green ivy, red poinsettias, and other plants that her mother had put in place. Jody would move a few things around and instantly create a much better look with her mom's approval.

The gifts the family exchanged were simple and often hand-crafted. Yet, all in all, no one was ever disappointed nor jealous of each other. Jody recalled the joy and excitement she felt when she saw Misty's expression on the Christmas morning that she found a guitar under the tree. She recalled that Nick was both elated and proud on the Christmas morning he was deemed mature enough to receive his first rifle.

Every year without fail, Christmas was special at the Newman home. And every year, Jody's heart would thump in excitement when the Christmas Season began to roll around. They were a loving and happy family throughout the year, but something special, something unique, happened at Christmastime. The music being played changed. The decorations throughout the cabin changed. Her mom replaced the family plates, cups, glasses, and bowls, with those bearing some design that referred to Christmas. Colored lights were hanging both inside the cabin and outside. Mom began baking more. Jody's parents made some extra shopping trips, including some made without the children. Songs, playing just about everywhere Jody went, proclaimed the soon arrival of Christmas and declared the season as the most wonderful time of the year.

Jody was lying in bed with her eyes wide open and her mind racing with a myriad of thoughts.

And I bought into all of that for years. I got that same warm and fuzzy feeling and those same butterflies dancing throughout my body every year as Christmas Day approached.

And then one day, I'm not even sure when it happened, it was all gone. Everything—even the story and significance of the Nativity. Christmas to me became nothing more than any other day, except now I attend holiday parties that are of value in generating business contacts and opportunities. Being back home again in Wyoming has caused me to reflect on Christmas and even recall some of the positive memories of times past, but those days are locked away somewhere in a used-to-be world. They had something to do with a Jody Newman who no longer exists. I'm not that person any more and I can't fake it and act like I believe in something that I don't. And even if I wanted to get any of it back, I don't know how. I have no idea whatsoever when and how I lost it all.

The man was tucked away in an old hunting cabin situated on five acres of land with no neighbors for miles. The place was so remote, most people did not even know it existed. The acreage it was situated on looked no different than the surrounding forest. Over the years, he was seen in the distance wandering alone in the woods at dusk by a few hunters. No one ever got a good look at his face. The man never spoke to anyone at all. Except when making purchases in town, he had not spoken a word to a single human being since the day he returned to the area eight years ago. Prior to that, he spent more than a dozen years behind prison bars. None of this was an issue to him. He possessed no need for human companionship. People would never understand or be comfortable with him anyway. He'd killed. If he had it to do over, he'd likely kill again. Repentance had never been a factor with him and he refused to be a hypocrite and pretend that he was remorseful over what he had done.

Recently, he heard the sounds of a woman screaming, crying out for help. It sent chills throughout his body. He knew it was not a woman. It was the sound of a cougar. Over the past few days, he'd seen tracks and came upon a few small animal kills. Hah! Guess he was not the only killer roaming the woods at night.

CHAPTER FIVE

Oh, Ho, the Mistletoe

[December 22]

"It's an open-house Christmas luncheon at the home of Sheriff Roy Holliday and his wife, Laura," Jolene said. She was sitting with Jody discussing the event that the sheriff held each year at his home. "Lot of the folks say it's a political deal that the sheriff conducts to keep voters aware of him," Jolene said followed by a chuckle. "But, he doesn't just do it at a Christmas prior to the next election year. He does it every year. And, besides, he's a very popular sheriff who doesn't need to throw a party to get people thinking about him."

Roy Holliday was in his fourth term as Park County Sheriff and would be running again in the fall of next year. The county included the Newman family among its nearly 30,000 residents and contained the majority of the total area of Yellowstone National Park. With a population of nearly 10,000 residents, Cody, governed by a city council and mayor, was the county's largest city. It was also where the headquarters for the Sheriff's Department was located.

Holliday was born and raised in Cody. He earned his degree in criminal justice at the University of Wyoming in Laramie and worked his way up the ranks within the Park County Sheriff Department. At forty-two years old, Holliday's body was still lean and tight. He had a moustache, salt and pepper hair, and blue eyes. He had a reputation for being a stern, but fair, lawman, who worked hard to provide preventative measures through his department that would proactively keep the area safe. The county had seen a decrease in crime in each of the seven years since he'd been in office.

Roy and Laura had two daughters, Amanda, a junior in high school, and Adrianna, who was a sophomore.

"I don't see our primary job as arresting people," Holliday often said. "Our job is to work hard with others throughout our community to build a positive and safe environment for all of us who live in Park County."

Jolene handed a fresh cup of coffee to Jody before asking her a question.

"Jody, would you be willing to go to Sheriff Roy's barbecue with me today? It's a casual event, you can come and go as you please, and the food is really good, especially the barbecue he grills."

"Okay, Mama," Jody said. "I'll go. Sounds pleasant enough."

Jody could see the excitement in her mom. As a proud mother, she wanted her neighbors to see her daughter.

Wow! How different and nice to have someone proud of me not because of what I've done or how much revenue I've generated, but simply because of who I am.

Forrest would stop in later. Nick was at work. Misty would stay home with the twins. So, Jody was going with her mother and Lana.

Sheriff Roy and his wife had a home on three acres of land within the city limits of Cody. When Jody arrived, Roy Holliday was wearing a chef's apron and greeting folks while remaining close to the grill and keeping a watchful eye on his barbecued beef, pork, and chicken. County Commissioner Chairman, Bert Manford, was seated nearby with a cold beer in his hand and a Santa Claus hat atop his head. The County Commissioners constitute the governing board of Park County. They manage the county's business concerns, approve budgets for the various county departments, and set the salaries and policies.

Mary Lynn Richfeld, the county Vice Chairwoman, was nearby, chatting with a group of women responsible for organizing and working with volunteers who Mary Lynn referrred to as the "life-blood" of the community.

School superintendents, principals, teachers, even school janitors showed up. Deputies on Holliday's force came and went. Some were off-duty. Others used a stop at the sheriff's home as a lunch break. And a good number of Park County's everyday folks dropped in throughout the time that Jody was there. Jody was getting a good look at a cross-section of the community.

Everyone that Jody met was cordial and kind towards her, but her conversations with them pretty much fell flat. Upon learning that she lived in New York, a few acknowledged that they'd been there. No one said they'd prefer to live there. When Jody mentioned the work she was engaged in, folks smiled, nodded their heads, but they had nothing more to say or add to a conversation about an industry they neither knew much about nor particularly were enraptured with. No one was ever the least bit snooty. No one was ever critical. Most of the people she chatted with simply didn't have enough exposure to or familiarity with the fashion or sportswear industry to engage in any meaningful discussions about it.

For some, their point of reference was the fact that they knew and respected Forrest and Jolene Newman. Jody met one of Misty's teachers and someone who worked with Nick at the dude ranch where he was employed. She spoke with a deputy who playfully acknowtedged having given a speeding ticket to Nick. She met a woman who was Lana's aunt.

When Jody caught sight of one of the young deputies in uniform who entered the Sheriff's home, she felt a prickling of her scalp and a quiver in her stomach. She slumped in her chair and attempted to evade notice. Her face was flushed. She once had a special friendship with Keith Hughes that began when they were elementary school classmates. In high school, Keith was the starting quarterback on the football team and top scorer on the varsity basketball team. Most of the girls also considered Keith, listed at six foot one with dark brown hair and blue eyes, to be the best-looking guy in the senior graduating class.

Back then, Jody regarded Keith as her best friend and he undoubtedly felt the same about her. They spent a great deal of time horseback riding and enjoying the outdoors, especially before winter moved in. Keith had a deep sensitivity to nature itself. He took the time to study and learn and knew most every tree and plant in the area. Keith also knew the identity of and nature of the animals in the East Yellowstone Valley. He could build fires from scratch, construct a shelter from materials available in the wild, and had outstanding survival skills.

The friendship Jody and Keith shared grew into a budding romance. Keith was the first boy Jody ever kissed. They attended their sophomore hop and senior prom together.

Jody and Keith also spent a great deal of time at each other's family home during Christmas. As a result, there was a time when it would have been impossible for Jody to think of Christmas without also thinking of Keith. In recent years, Jody had somehow successfully expunged those memories.

When Jody announced that she would be attending Oregon State University on a full scholarship, things began to get a bit strained between them.

"It's only about a seventeen hour drive from here," Jody said, as if that was not a big deal. "Besides, I've been offered a free ride to pursue a degree in the very thing that I want to do in my life."

At first, Jody communicated quite often with Keith, but then she faded in her relationship with him. It wasn't another guy that drew her away from her high school sweetheart. She had different aspirations and future goals than Keith. She had already moved on with her life.

Keith spotted Jody as he walked in Sheriff Holliday's home and made the first move when he walked up and greeted her.

"Hi, Jody. Heard that you were in the area," Keith said.

Jody smiled and extended her hand in greeting.

"Well, I must say that's rather incredible since I only arrived here yesterday and didn't know in advance I'd be coming here."

She laughed at her own response. Keith laughed along with her.

"Well, excuse me, dear," Keith said, "but have you forgotten? Here in East Yellowstone Valley, before the telegraph, telephone, cell phones, or the Internet, we had this thing called word-of-mouth. It still exists and, so far, nothing has been able to top its speed and the number of people it can reach in the shortest period of time."

Jody and Keith both laughed. Jody made a concerted effort not to stare at her old boyfriend, though, if it was even possible, he was even more handsome than he had been as a teenager.

"I didn't know you joined the Sheriff's Department, Keith."

"Yeah, well, it took me some time before I was willing to admit that my future in athletics was limited. They listed me as being six feet two inches tall, when I am actually about a quarter of an inch above six feet. At that height, I'd be too short for a starting quarterback or basketball guard at a major college level, unless I had exceptional skills, which I did not. So, I took a basketball scholarship offer and spent two years in Powell at Northwest College. Then, I finished up at the University of Wyoming earning a degree in criminal justice."

"I always knew you were college material, Keith, but you were so negative when I accepted a scholarship to Oregon State," Jody said.

"That whole situation came across wrong. I was actually proud of you, but I just couldn't handle you being so far away. I was afraid I would lose you, which I did. It doesn't matter now. You were right. I was wrong. And I'm so proud of you for what you've accomplished."

Jody was surprised at how easily Keith addressed that entire situation. He didn't pull any punches. He offered no excuses or justifications. She wished that they would have resolved things this way back then...

No, she paused long enough to reconsider her train of thought. Things would have ended up as they did. She wanted New York, glamour, unlimited opportunities and Keith would have had none of that to offer.

Even so, her reaction to Keith now surprised her.

CHAPTER SIX

Tis the Season To Be Jolly

[December 22]

The morning sun was awakening, stretching, yawning, and sending out an array of orange, yellow, and pink colors that reflected off the snow and ice. Jody rose from her bed and peered out the window in time to spot a small herd of deer grazing on an open bale or two of hay that her father had placed closer to the woods.

Hmm... such a beautiful morning, I must admit. And my Papa placed that hay there for the deer. No profit, no gain in feeding wildlife, but he does it anyway.

I slept so well last night. I already feel refreshed and I've only been here one day. Well, what do you expect when you had a day of flying out west, followed by a night of family activities. There's no magic in sleeping out in the boonies. This place is still in the middle of nowhere.

Jody hopped back in the bed and was lying down when she heard the knock on her bedroom door and called for whoever it was to come in.

Rusty and Rylie had been told by their mom to knock before entering their big sister's room. They ran to the bed and hopped in, giggling and all smiles as they snuggled with Jody.

"It's only three days before Christmas," Rusty said. "We can't wait."

"Yeah," Rylie said, "and me and Rusty have presents for you that we put under the tree. We can't wait until you open 'em."

"That's right," Rusty said, "but no peeking. Ya gotta wait 'til Christmas morning. That's the rules around here."

Jody's chuckle was cut short at the thought that she would not be here Christmas morning. She would be in New York meeting with potential clients who liked her product line.

"I'm so happy you're here with us," Rylie said, as she reached over and hugged Jody.

"Me, too, " Rusty said. "Makes Christmas better. Wish you always lived here."

"Why you gotta live in new yawk, anyway?" Rylie asked.

Jody smiled.

"Well, New York is where my job is."

"You got a horse there?" Rusty asked.

"No," Jody said patting Rusty on his head. "No horse there."

"They got Christmas in new wawk?" Riley asked.

"Oh, yes, they do have Christmas there."

Even as Jody uttered those words, her mind traveled along a path she would never say aloud to her little brother and sister.

But not for me. The City is inundated with evidences of the Holiday Season everywhere you go. But I've avoided everything for years.

Jody threw on a sweatshirt and jogging pants and entered the kitchen area where her mom was cooking eggs, bacon, and biscuits. The smile on Jolene's face as she greeted her daughter almost brought Jody to tears. She'd choose a time to reveal her early departure, but not at the start of the day.

"Coffee's fresh, darling," her mom sang out, "and we'll have some breakfast for you in just a few."

Nick was already at work, her dad was somewhere outside on the property, so she had breakfast with her mom, Misty, and the twins.

Jody's phone buzzed signaling the arrival of another text.

Plan to arrive at the office at 7:45 a.m. for some preliminary discussion in advance of the meeting with SAIKO. —AdMon

Jody responded with a "will do" and poured a cup of coffee for herself. She was surprised to hear a knock at the cabin door.

"Woohoo, it's just me," the voice sang out as a woman entered carrying a homemade carrot cake wrapped in cellophane paper with a red bow on top.

Jolene Newman hugged her neighbor and turned to Jody.

"Jody, you remember Cynthia Woods?"

"Jody, is that really you? My, my, you're as beautiful as ever."

"Thank you, Mrs. Woods. It's nice to see you again."

The women sat and drank coffee together, along with Jolene's homemade blueberry cupcakes. Jolene handed a pecan pie to Cynthia before she left.

Jolene turned to Jody and shrugged while a smile covered her face.

"It'll be like that all day today and tomorrow," Jolene said. "People will be dropping by with a little Christmas something. By now, the word has spread that my daughter's in from New York, so folks will come to me rather than have me traipse around while you're here. None of our neighbors are within sight of our home, but we all know one another.

Hmm, people who can't even see one another's home from where they live all know and respond to one another. Heck, I've got close to... I don't know, maybe a thousand tenants living in my apartment building and I don't know even one of them. Well, I do say hello to old Mrs. Mullins or is her name Muller? Anyway, she lives in the apartment next to me. Guess the only people I know in New York are Roxi and the people I work with.

Colonel Connor Harrelson was the Sherrif Department spokesperson, media specialist, and Search and Rescue Coordinator. Prior to joining the Park County Department, Harrelson was with the Gallatin County Sheriff's Department in Montana for twenty-two years. He ended his career there as a trainer for the Big Sky Search and Rescue members.

Harrelson and Sheriff Holliday were sitting together in Holliday's office with steaming cups of coffee.

"Alrighty then, Connor," the sheriff said, "all the latest weather reports are predicting a major winter storm headed our way within the next day or so. Update me, please, on where we're at with the preventative and preparatory steps we've taken."

"Well," Harrelson began, "we've been putting out public notices throughout the area by every means possible, including reminding people of the safety precautions and preparatory steps they need to take. All emergency vessels—helicopters, all-terrain vehicles, and snowmobiles have been checked and are ready to go at a moment's notice. I've been in constant touch with Ted Logan and he assures me that our horses and equestrian team members are also ready."

The sheriff took a sip of coffee, wiped his lips with his shirt sleeve, and placed the cup back down on his desk.

"Excellent, sounds great, Connor. Hopefully, we won't be needing to do a search and rescue, but you know how it is. No matter how much advanced warning we give, seems we always end up with people who don't give heed and end up in trouble somewhere."

Following a light lunch, Forrest invited Jody and Misty to go horseback riding with him.

"Can't possibly remember the last time I went riding with my two daughters," Forrest said. "I love the idea of just being with you two, while at the same time, I've got a calf that wandered off and never made it back. We can look for her while we're enjoying the countryside."

He turned towards Jody and grinned.

"I'm assumin' my big-city girl still knows how to ride a horse."

Jody nodded her head.

"Some things you never forget, Papa," she said.

Funny—in the city they'd say you never forget how to ride a bicycle. Here, we say the same thing about riding a horse. It's interesting that something I did just about every day while growing up is now something I haven't done in years.

The radiant sun had no impact upon the freezing temperatures. The blue sky served as a temporary deception that a major storm was headed their way. As they rode the sure-footed horses through the snow, Jody was enraptured by the beauty of the area they traveled through. She stared out at open fields draped in untouched snow, pockets of wooded areas thick with dark green pine trees, scattered shrubbery, and small animals scurrying about gathering last-minute provisions before they'd be hunkered down riding out an onslaught of inclement weather. Jody marveled at the hills and valleys comprising the foothills of the nearby Absaroka Range of the majestic Rocky Mountains. In addition to its natural beauty, everything out here appeared to be so fresh and clean.

Jody remembered when she was younger and her daddy would take her on long horseback rides throughout the area. Sometimes Nick came along with them. They brought along food so they could stop somewhere and picnic together. The countryside was breathtaking, the times of being with her daddy and brother were priceless. Yet, somehow along with so much more, those were times and memories she lost somehow, somewhere along the way. She rode the subway now, spending a great deal of time in dark tunnels. She traveled in taxi cabs being tossed about by a driver with a heavy foot and lane changes that ignored every semblance of safety and sensitivity to a passenger.

They rode for about forty-five minutes when Forrest spotted the calf—or what was left of her. Jody and Misty pulled their horses closer and stared at the bovine remains.

"Grizzly, Papa?" Misty asked.

"No, those aren't bear tracks. Looks like a big cat has wandered into the area. They generally never come down this far. The cats usually stay up in the hills. When an animal ventures out of its normal environment, it means they're desperate. This'll get more attention from the ranchers around here than even a grizzly bear would."

Jody's face turned ashen and she gripped the horse's reins so tight that her knuckles were white. She'd been born and raised in this area, but it had been years since she even thought about the dangers of a cougar or grizzly.

"Are animals like bears or cougars becoming more of a genuine threat to humans around here?" Jody asked.

"Well, they generally won't mess with a human, but we always have to respect them and give them their space. When they're forced out of their environment, they become a greater threat to livestock. Someone injured or stranded at night in the woods or, perhaps, a child or small household pet would also be vulnerable to attack. In the nearly 150-year history of Yellowstone National Park, there have been less than ten, something like eight deaths, most likely caused by grizzlies."

Jody considered what her father had just said.

In New York City, we average about 15,000 robberies, over 30,000 assaults, and several hundred murders every year. Sounds as if you're better off dealing with bears than with humans.

"We need to head on back," Forrest said. "I need to let the others in this area know that we've got us a big cat prowling around, so they can take adequate precautions with their family members and their stock. You can be sure this here critter enjoyed its meal of beef and will be looking for more real soon."

CHAPTER SEVEN

Have Yourself a Merry Little Christmas

[December 22-23]

Jolene was right. Neighbors dropped by throughout the day, each one bringing something to give to the Newman family. From baked goods to homemade arts and crafts, everyone brought something original and received something back from Jolene. For Jody back in New York, exchanging gifts was a hassle, an obligatory activity that generated stress and confusion. Jody struggled with what to get someone while striving to remain within her budget. What Jody was seeing here was that people either spent a few days baking or time creating something often made of everyday items they gathered up from property around their homes. And, from the smiles on each person giving a gift, Jody could readily see that exchanging presents was not a burden at all. It was an enjoyable experience.

That night, following a luscious meal consisting of chicken and gravy, mashed potatoes, butter beans in a brown gravy, and corn, they all gathered again near the tree and the fireplace for a time of singing. Jolene sat at the piano and played the music for each song. Misty accompanied her mother with her guitar. Rusty and Rylie each had a small tamborine and did their very best to sometimes stay in tune with the songs. Lana, who was back at the cabin with Nick, also had a tamborine. She had no difficulty at all staying in sync with the music and singing.

Jody could not help but notice that everyone sang robustly and was fully engaged. There was nothing forced, nothing strained at all in the night's event. They were singing because they wanted to sing—they enjoyed doing so. Jody's thoughts ran rampant.

So many of the activities I engage in with others are contrived. It's like we do certain things because we're supposed to, because we want to look good in front of others, because we pretend that we like doing the things we do, when in reality, we do not.

But, Jody could plainly see that there was no pretense in her family members. Their hearts were in this thing called Christmas and, in addition to its religious significance, it was a season for joy, peace, and love.

Before she fell asleep that night, Jody started to book her return flight to New York. She found a flight that would depart at 5:24 p.m. and arrive at JFK Airport at 11:44 p.m. The fare was in excess of $1,000, but she was charging it to her company. She hesitated several times before finalizing her booking. A wave of guilt pressed against her mind. She knew that her family would be disappointed. Then again, they didn't understand the life she now lived. It was as foreign to them as their lives and values now were to her.

Jody sighed deeply, pressed her lips together in a slight grimace, and booked the flight. The clock would strike midnight on Christmas morning in New York before she ever left the airport, giving her ample time for the meeting some seven hours later. She sent the flight details to Alfred Monmouth and closed her eyes. Tomorrow, December 23, would be her last full day in Wyoming.

❧

There was no morning sun to greet them the next day. The sky was overcast in solid whiteness, indicating that it was pregnant with snow. The winds were already more active, causing the tops of the trees to sway. Sometime later in the day, a fierce winter storm would arrive.

Despite the impending storm, or maybe because of it, more neighbors came by on this day. Whatever effect storms like this had on the people in this region, they certainly did not diminish their Christmas spirit. Each person bore the same smiles and cheerfulness and had plenty of hugs to share. Storms in the city where Jody lived served to cripple transportation and generate delays and confusion. Storms here in Wyoming were common enough for people to simply make adjustments and continue on with their day.

Forrest Newman made a mental checklist of things he needed to do before the storm hit. The list was not all that long, since he already had most things secure and aligned with freezing temperatures. Throughout the day, as the sun remained cloistered behind overcast skies and the winds became stronger, Forrest increased the sticks of wood for the wood burning stove and logs for the fireplace. Jolene made an extra stew and a lentil soup. Nick was busy at work doing preventative things to further protect the animals there.

❧

The news of a big cat prowling through the area spread quickly. The threat was exacerbated when Farber Johnson found one of his sheep slaughtered and the tracks at the scene belonged to a cougar. Justus Richardson said something had his entire corral of horses spooked one night, but he never did spot what it was. The tracks he identified in the morning revealed it was the big cat. As a result of all this, Ned Wilkinson was attempting to round up a team to hunt the animal down.

Late that afternoon, one of the mares at the Newman ranch chose that time to foal. She was in the barn along with the other horses. Forrest, Jolene, Jody, and Misty all gathered together to assist and witness the birth. Rusty and Rylie were also in the barn playing nearby as the others attended to the mare.

"So far, so good," Forrest exclaimed as he appraised the mare's condition. "Looks like the foal is not in breach and mama is breathing well. It won't be long now. Needless to say, she might've picked a better day when it comes to the weather, but horses don't seem to pay that no mind."

"Heck, neither do humans when you stop and think about it," Jolene said.

Everyone laughed.

The adults were all focused on the mare when Rusty and Rylie spotted a rabbit in a nest of hay in the barn. Their little eyes were bulging and smiles covered their faces when they saw that the rabbit had little babies tucked all around her. The bunny, startled by the children, began to hop away in an effort to distract them from her babies. She headed outside the barn and the twins followed.

"We gots to catch the bunny," Rusty said, "or she might freeze in the cold."

"Yeah, then her babies won't have their mama," Rylie said.

The rabbit ran into the woods and twins pursued. The rabbit ran faster and the twins ran as fast as their little legs could carry them. They went deeper and deeper into the woods, unaware of how far they had traveled.

The combination of an overcast sky and a tree-filled forest created a darkness that both frightened and confused the children. When Rylie began to cry, Rusty took her hand.

"Don't cry Rylie and don't be scared. I'll get us out of these woods."

When Rusty heard rustling sounds in the nearby brush, he was convinced that someone or something was following them. It sounded like a person or maybe it was a bear. Also, he wasn't supposed to hear his daddy talking about a cougar roaming in the woods, but he did overhear that.

"C'mon, Rylie, we gots to go faster," he said, though in an effort to not frighten Rylie, he never told her why. He held tight to Rylie's little hand and, once again, began to run. They ran without looking back or considering how far they had gone. Rusty was frightened, but he felt good that he was leading his sister through the woods and away from danger. He did not know that he was leading them both deeper in and farther away from their home.

⨏

Misty was the first to notice that Rusty and Rylie were no longer in the barn. She stepped outside looking for them, but they were nowhere in sight. Misty quickly went inside the cabin searching for them only to learn they were not there either. She began to call out for them, but did not receive an answer. Misty's face turned ashen. For a moment, she froze, feeling rooted to the spot where she stood. Images of what-could-be already began to flash through her mind as she stared out at the dark woods. The snow was falling heavier now, the wind was blowing harder, and the temperature was dropping.

Little footprints headed into the woods caused Misty to tremble. She broke free from the stupor she was in and ran to the barn.

"Papa, Mama... Rusty and Riley... they're gone..." Misty began to sob. "I-I c-can't find them anywhere."

CHAPTER EIGHT

Please Come Home for Christmas

[December 23]

Forrest ran as fast as he could into the woods. Jolene, Jody, and Misty waited, expecting he'd be back in a few minutes with the two children. But, when Forrest returned, his jaw was clenched and his hands were tightened into fists.

"There's no sign of them," Forrest said. "It'll be dark soon. We need help now."

Within minutes, they had a plan of action. Forrest would go back into the woods on horseback. Misty would take a horse to Ned Wilkinson's place. Ned was an auxiliary deputy who was the best contact into the Sheriff's Department. Jolene would take the family Jeep to the nearest neighbor to help generate a neighborhood alert. Jody would remain at the cabin to be available once people began to arrive.

And arrive they did! Even before the sheriff's deputies and the Search and Rescue Team got there, neighbors Farber Johnson, Eddie Grant, Justus Richardson, Ned Wilkinson, and Little Roy Wilkins were all on the scene. And, Jody would soon see more neighbors headed their way. Nick showed up with a few of his co-workers. He ran up to Jody and hugged her tightly as they wept together. Then, he and the others rode their horses into the woods.

Yellowstone Snowmobiles and Equipment showed up with a truck carrying extra snowmobiles to assist searchers. Wilbur Highwater drove in with a trailer containing a few horses that were saddled and ready to go as needed. Eddie Farthings brought several tactical flashlights for searchers to use in the woods.

"These babies will shine their light forever," Eddie said. "Wanda criticized me every time I bought a new one. Said I'm a techie-junkie, she did. But, I've always watched for the sales and figured they'd come in handy one day. Brought a few bullhorns, also."

Colonel Connor Harrelson, the Search and Rescue Coordinator, arrived in an SUV along with his wife, Rita. Members of his team were also quickly showing up. Harrelson organized them into smaller groups, arranged for the areas each would cover, and had them reporting in to him by radio every fifteen minutes. They had men and woman on foot and in all-terrain vehicles. The vehicles and snowmobiles would be limited because of the thickness of the forest. Helicopters could not be utilized due to the high winds and limited visibility.

Ted Logan's equestrian team members arrived, some on horseback, some pulling a horse in a trailer due to their original distance from the Newman cabin. Logan quickly had them organized and on the go.

Harrelson reported in by radio to Sheriff Holliday who was on his way.

"Watcha got for me, Connor?" the Sheriff asked.

"Initial tracks confirm the little ones did go into the woods, but with them being so small and lightweight they don't leave much of a track. Add the new-fallen snow, which is still coming down heavily, and we've already lost the ability to rely on their tracks. I've got Dick Coleman on his way with his dogs."

"Roger that," Holliday said. "Keep me in the loop. I'm on the way."

⁓

Jody stood transfixed by all the activity. Her body was trembling. Her heart was racing so fast, she felt as if it would burst. Her eyes bore a dazed look as she witnessed the blur of activity all around her. As a result, she didn't even notice at first when Keith Hughes, walking with his horse, approached her. He was dressed in uniform as a sheriff's deputy.

When she spotted him, tears, like large crystal globules began rolling down both cheeks.

Keith leaned over, smiled, hugged her, and spoke calmly to her.

"Hi, Jody. Hey, listen to me. We're going to find your little brother and sister. Don't you worry about that."

Jody's body trembled as she held tight to Keith. She looked up into his eyes.

"Keith... oh, Keith... they're s-so young and it's... it's so c-cold and... th-there are dangerous animals w-wandering..."

Keith gently placed a finger over Jody's lips and smiled.

"No, don't even go there, Jody. Stop."

Keith reached down and lifted Jody's chin. As he gazed into her eyes, he could sense the fear and grief that encompassed her.

"Listen to me, Jody. Like I said, we're going to find Rusty and Riley. I promise you. I won't quit searching until we've got them back home safe and sound."

Jody placed her head against Keith's chest and sobbed. Her speech was interrupted by sobs and sighs.

"Oh... K-Keith... it-it w-will take a... a m-miracle."

"Hey," Keith said with a smile on his face. "I'm okay with that, Jody. I haven't lost my belief in miracles and Christmas is the perfect time of the year for them."

Jody continued to stare into Keith's eyes. As she did, he smiled once again and wiped her tears with his finger.

"I promise you," Keith said again. Then, he smiled, turned away, and linked up with the Search and Rescue team where he was one of the teamleaders who would report directly into Connor Harrelson.

Jolene and Misty were now standing with Jody in the midst of all the activity. Two local ambulances were on the scene prepared to assist, as needed. A reporter from the Cody Enterprise newspaper, another from the Powell Tribune were on the scene. Jody could see a television media truck approaching, also.

Jolene remained calm hiding the anguish she was feeling. Lana was standing with Jolene's arm wrapped around her. Misty was sobbing and Jody was numb, staring out as she held Misty in her arms.

Jody watched as Reverend Watkins gathered a group in a circle and led them in a short prayer before they joined the others in the search for Rusty and Rylie. She bowed her head and tried to think of something to say. Jody could not remember the last time she prayed.

Neighbors continued to pour into the area, but they did not come to gawk and watch the activity. Men, carrying weapons and flashlights, joined in the search. Women bore breads, baked goods, paper cups, and ingredients needed for hot drinks. Everyone who arrived came to help in some way.

The women convinced Jolene, Jody, Lana, and Misty to step back inside the cabin, got each of them a hot drink, and did their best to maintain a positive flow of conversation.

Sheriff Holliday was now at the Newman home. He entered the house to speak with Jolene, Jody, and Misty, assuring them that they were doing everything possible to find Rusty and Rylie. He then returned outside to his car where he could better communicate with the search teams without anyone else hearing their conversations.

Connor Harrelson checked in with Sheriff Holliday.

"Our guys are already farther in than we expected two little five-year-olds could travel in this weather, Roy. And still no sign of 'em. Gotta say, I'm surprised. Best I can come up with, they got themselves turned around and have ended up traveling quite a ways from their home."

The air was cold, hard, and biting.

"Man, this storm is brutal. Give me your analysis, Connor," Holliday said.

Harrelson paused for a moment before speaking. He had learned over the years to never respond in a crisis situation with words of despair that could serve to discourage people in the field. Even though he was only speaking to the sheriff, he would maintain that standard. Yet, at the same time, he wanted to provide the sheriff with all that they were up against.

"In this weather," Harrelson responded, "the time we have is limited before these young ones end up in big trouble. Since the normal body core temperature is 98.6 degrees Fahrenheit, mild hypothermia will set in at about 95. After that is when the really bad things begin to happen. We're talking amnesia at 91 degrees, a loss of consciouness at 82, and death can occur at anything below 70. Plus, we have the threat of severe frostbite."

"Sounds like a small window of opportunity getting even smaller every minute," the sheriff said.

"Yeah, I'm afraid so," Harrelson responded, " and we've got another major problem, Roy. We've got reports of a rogue cougar in the area."

Sheriff Holliday was a former marine who dealt with some tough situations before he joined the Park County Sheriff's Department. But, at the mention of a big cat in the area, he was struggling against thinking about the worst possible outcome.

"We've got to find those little ones now, Connor. They've got to be somewhere. They couldn't have just disappeared. Dear God, we need to find them before it's too late."

⸂⸃

Darkness was moving in quickly. Bright flashlights could be seen throughout the woods.

The howling wind was getting louder. Falling snow and crystals of ice made it increasingly difficult to see.

Vincent J. Sachar

Were it not for his excellent tracking skills, Keith could easily have missed spotting the faint human tracks that were leading in a direction away from all the other searchers in the woods. He attempted to inform the others that he was pulling away from them, but he was unable to transmit anything on his radio.

After traveling for about thirty minutes or so, he came upon something that turned his face ashen and lifted the hair on his nape and arms. His range of vision was limited, but what he saw was a small pack of wolves grouped together around something lying on the ground. Despite the winds, Keith could hear the snarls, growls, snaps, and yips of the wolves as they fought against each other tearing at whatever they had found. Keith spurred his horse towards the wolves. The horse clearly indicating its displeasure at approaching wolves, nevertheless, obeyed the commands of its master.

Keith's chest was gripped with a tightness that made him feel nauseous. His body was trembling. Despite the fact that he was still young, Keith Hughes was reputed to be one of the best outdoorsmen in the county. His tracking skills were excellent. His knowledge of the outdoors and his survival skills were well-beyond his age. But, this was something that went beyond skills and Keith was still shaking as he made his approach.

"Dear, God… no, please… no," he muttered in what was no more than a whisper.

When he arrived at the scene, he withdrew his handgun and fired a shot causing the wolves to temporarily leave. They remained nearby snarling and baring their teeth. Keith looked down at the ground and blew out a burst of air.

55

"Oh, okay now," Hughes mumbled to himself. He paused and took another deep breath. "a deer, it-it's just the remains of a deer that had been caught in a hand-made trap of some sort."

But as Keith examined the area closer, he could see the initial kill was not made by wolves. He spotted the tracks of a cougar.

Hmm, looks like the big cat made the kill, but the pack of wolves chased the cougar away. There were no signs of the children.

Despair and hopelessness were striking the hearts of the searchers. The snow was mixed with particles of ice. The temperature was continually dropping. The winds were blowing harder. Without the aid of a moon overhead, it was now pitch black. Protocol required that the teams be called back in for their own safety. The Newman family did not yet know that the search would be called off for the night. Sheriff Holliday would carry that message to them after all else was cleared with the search teams.

Connor Harrelson had two daunting tasks to carry out. The first would be to contact all the rescue team personnel and terminate all search activity immediately. The second would be to sound as if resuming the search at daybreak carries with it any actual possibility that these two little children could survive a night in a freezing winter storm and found alive the following day.

Harrelson made the call ordering everyone to return to the Newman property at once. All of the team leaders, other than Keith Hughes, responded acknowledging Harrelson's command.

Vincent J. Sachar

It was moments later when Hughes called in using another line so that all the others would not be privy to his call.

"Sergeant Hughes calling Colonel Harrelson. This is Sergeant Hughes. Do you read me, Colonel?"

"Go ahead, Keith. I hear you, son," Harrelson said.

Hughes breathed a sigh of relief upon receiving confirmation that his radio transmission had been successful.

"Keith, this is Sheriff Roy. I'm on, also."

Keith's voice was tight, evidencing the biting cold temperatures he was in and the urgency he felt in the need to find the twins.

"I ended up due east from the others and have traveled another mile. I spotted faint tracks, human tracks, that I only noticed when some of them were under a tree or tall bush. In fact, they're likely covered up by now. I recently came across the carcass of a deer caught in a man-made trap. Someone's out here. Based upon the print size, we're talking about a male with a size ten foot. This person may have nothing to do with the missing children, but, I'm requesting permission to remain out here and see what this is all about."

Although Harrelson was Keith Hughes' direct superior, the sheriff had the ultimate authority over everyone. There was a long pause before any words were spoken.

Hughes broke the silence.

"Gentlemen, I'm all we've got left tonight. I'm the only search team member anywhere out here. If someone has these children, we need to know."

When Sheriff Holliday did respond, he spoke directly to Connor Harrelson, even though Keith Hughes would still be able to hear what was being said.

"Connor, I'm inclined to let Keith go ahead with this. Your thoughts?"

"I'm okay with it, Roy. But, I've been thinking. We don't have a record of anyone ever living out that far in that area of the woods. Concerns me just who those tracks may belong to. And where would he be staying in weather like this?"

And, in that moment of time, Roy Holliday thought he might know. A bolt of fear raced through his body. Could it really be? After all these years?

CHAPTER NINE

Sleep Well, Little Children, Wherever You Are

[December 23]

"Keith, Connor, hold on. I'll be back with you both as quickly as possible." Then Holliday disconnected from the radio and made a call into his departmental dispatch with his cell phone. The dispatcher on duty was Janet Overbee.

"Hey, Sheriff, everything okay?" Janet said.

"Hi, Janet. Excuse my abruptness, but I'm in a real hurry here. We got anybody in the office?"

"Indeed, we do, sir. Detective Floyd is in. Would take more'n a blizzard to keep him away, eh? You want I should connect you with him?"

"Please, Janet. Thanks."

Randall Floyd had been with the Park County Sheriff's Department longer than Roy Holliday. Janet Overbee was right. It was a common joke around the office that Floyd should have a bed in his office, since he was always in the building. Floyd answered quickly.

"Randall, this is Roy."

"Hey, Roy, how's the search and rescue going?"

"Still working at it, Floyd. Listen, I need something and need it as quickly as possible."

"Shoot, I'm ready."

"Caleb Banks. Anything new on him? On his status?"

"Hmm, Doc Banks," Floyd said. "You're going back a lifetime there. Ain't never heard anything since they sent him away. Hold on, Roy, let me make a quick check for you."

With Keith Hughes still out in freezing weather on horseback in a dark forest and Connor Harrelson and Roy Holliday waiting, every minute seemed like forever, but Floyd was back on the line in a relatively short amount of time.

"Hey, Roy, ain't sure why we never got the notice we were entitled to receive, but Caleb Banks was released from prison just shy of eight years ago. There's no record of where he is now and whether he's even still alive. Best I can tell, the man would be about seventy-years-old now."

"Thanks, Floyd, gotta run. We'll talk more about this later."

Randall Floyd's news sent a shot of adrenaline through Holliday's body. He called back into Harrelson and Hughes.

"Connor, Keith, think we might know who those tracks belong to. Name's Caleb Banks. Keith, the man's a convicted murderer. This changes everything."

Connor Harrelson responded quickly. His voice evidenced his concern.

"Hey, Roy. Seems to me we need to get Keith back in here now. We can't have him out there alone with a convicted murderer out there—a man who's been hidden away deep in the woods for years."

Keith interrupted. Holliday and Harrelson had difficulty hearing Keith at times, as the howling winds blew heavily in spurts and drowned out Keith's voice.

"I'm a long ways into these woods," Keith said. "I'm the only person in position to see if the children have been abducted by a killer. If there's any chance they're still alive, we've got to do something now. If I encounter this man, I can defend myself. Two little children don't have a chance against him. I've got to at least try to find and save them—if there's any chance at all.

Jody slipped off away from everyone else and went inside her bedroom. She sat on the bed and sobbed. She cried harder than ever before in her life. She wept so much that her ribs ached, her face hurt, and, most significantly, her heart was totally shattered.

No one had mentioned anything about the search teams coming back in for the night, but Jody knew it was not possible for them to continue in this weather. The wind was increasingly fierce. Snow and sleet continued to fall and, along with the darkness, eradicated all visibility. The freezing temperatures cut right through clothing, scarves, gloves, boots, and head coverings. Jody was sure that two little five-year-old children could not possibly survive a night like this outdoors and alone.

She continued to picture Rusty and Rylie in her mind.

Oh my God! Oh my Lord! They're so young, so fragile. Just hours ago, Rusty and Rylie were sky high, so excited about Christmas morning and now... now they're gone. I treated

Christmas as if it were nothing—just a big waste of time, something that provided no measurable benefit to me. I didn't see the joy and love it helped to generate. I forgot how it helped young people to set their imaginations in force.

My God, Oh my God... Christmas morning to me was going to be a meeting with Japanese buyers in a Manhattan office. I have a flight booked for tomorrow that I never told my family about.

Jody tried to stop crying and gain control over the ache in her heart. She tried to block out picturing her brother and sister, but she could not. She wept, first and foremost, for Rusty and Rylie. She wept for her Dad, Mom, Nick, Lana, and Misty. Then, she wept for herself and for what she had allowed herself to become.

∽

"Caleb Banks grew up in this area," Sheriff Holliday said, speaking by radio to Harrelson. "Sadly, he was a victim of an abusive father, a heavy drinker who also abused Caleb's mom. Beat the mother one night until she ended up in a coma for the remainder of her life. Caleb ended up living with an aunt and uncle somewhere in Montana, I believe. He was intelligent and an achiever. Long story short, he graduated college, ended up in med school, and became a physician—an internist, I believe.

He came back to Wyoming. Lived over in Laramie, but had a hunter's cabin built somewhere in this area.

The details are kind of sketchy to me and I didn't have time to run through the file with Floyd. All I remember is the case involved the deaths of a woman, a child, and another doctor."

"Is Banks a threat?" Harrelson asked.

Vincent J. Sachar

"Don't know," Holliday answered. "Can a leopard change its spots? We could be dealing with a bitter, twisted man, capable of killing again, maybe because he feels he was dealt a wrong hand by our justice system. Keith, I can't risk your safety, even though... "

"Sheriff Roy," Keith interjected, "I have my weapon. I'll be extremely cautious. I give you my word on that. Please, just let me finish this out. Please."

Once again, the silence was deafening. Harrelson said nothing. The ball was clearly in Holliday's court. Keith sat quietly with his heart beating fast. Something in his inner gut, something instinctively, was telling him that he needed to follow this up.

Sheriff Holliday spoke slowly as if he was making decisions even as he spoke.

"Now you listen here, Keith, and listen good. The man you may be dealing with is someone who gets out of prison and hides himself away deep in the woods. Nothing about that sounds good to me. Floyd said there was a rumor that Banks had an old hunting cabin somewhere out there. Can't be all that far from where you are now. There's got to be another way in there, but, quite frankly, it's a remote area. No telling how you get a vehicle in there. I've got Randall Floyd trying to find some old local hunter who might know. Meanwhile, I'm getting a small team, including myself, to start heading back out on horseback to your area. Wish I could find an EMT who'd be willing to ride out with us just in case Banks has kidnapped the children and they're not yet dead."

"Danny Clark," Keith said. "He's an EMT and a real outdoors guy. I've gone hunting and fishing with him a number of times and he's awesome."

"Okay, we'll call him," the sheriff said. "Now, again, you hear me, Keith. I don't want you taking any chances, son. If you see the situation requires backup, you wait for that backup. And don't trust this man. You hear me? That's an order Hughes, not a suggestion."

"Yes, sir," Keith said. "Copy that, sir."

⁓

Ted Logan took responsibility for contacting Danny Clark and had him over at the Newman's place in no time at all. Danny was told they might not find any sign of the twins when they reached the old man's cabin. They might not even find Caleb Banks.

"Hey, I'm in. Even the slightest chance is more than enough for me to go," Danny said. "Thanks for contacting me."

In the little time before he and others would head out again, Sheriff Holliday went into the cabin to speak with the Newman family members. He was gracious and said all the right things to the family, but his words all sounded so hollow. How could any of them believe that two little children have survived this many hours in a frozen forest also filled with life-threatening animals.

Holliday did not speak openly about Caleb Banks, but, he did mention to Forrest Newman that they were headed towards a remote hunting cabin. Forrest insisted that he and Nick go with the sheriff's team.

"Sure, Forrest, you and the boy can join us. If we find your children it'd be good to have you there. But, I have to know you'll both follow my orders and keep your emotions in check. We don't know exactly what we're dealing with and the safety of your little ones might very well be at stake."

Forrest agreed. He had been told there was a chance that the twins may have been abducted. Sheriff Holliday did not add that the abductor might be a convicted killer.

Keith Hughes rode in the blackness of the night relying upon his flashlight. He had taken every proper step to dress warmly, yet the cold cut right through his clothing and froze his body. He knew that he might already be a victim of frostnip, an early stage of frostbite, which meant he only had a limited time to get to some place warm.

I need to get out of this cold. Hah. Slim chance that's going to happen. Man, I've never been so cold in my life. I've got to find ways to ignore it. We've got two little ones out here somewhere and I need to do everything in my power to find them. I took this job because I wanted to be involved in saving lives. I wanted to make a difference. Well, Keith, my boy, now's your chance. Suck it up and press on.

Hah, I used to say that to myself during crucial moments in a high school football game. But, there's a whole lot more at stake here. This isn't a game.

Squalls of wind threw snow and ice into the air threatening to knock Keith out of his saddle. The bursts of wind were deafening. It was during one of the interludes when the wind was not roaring that Keith first heard a sound that startled him. He felt a chill traveling through his body as if an alarm was attempting to alert him to danger. He urged his horse forward. There it was again. He was being followed. Something was moving behind him, stalking him, converting him to prey, rather than predator. It was patient, moving slowly, its stealthy movements were designed to hide the fact that it was even there. But, Keith's strong survival skills were on full alert. His horse became increasingly jittery. He had to keep the animal from panicking. If the horse threw him and ran away, Keith had no chance at all to survive. Wind, snow, ice, whatever, both Keith and the horse knew that a predator was nearby.

This has got to be that cougar. A bear would not follow like this. Okay, gotta stay calm. I could be attacked at any minute and gotta keep my horse from getting totally spooked. Aren't freezing winds, snow, ice, and biting cold temperatures enough to deal with? Do I have to deal with a big cat that sees me and my horse as a next meal?

Keith turned his horse around and stared out at the area behind him. He had his gun drawn. Between the bursts of wind, he listened closely, but the sounds he heard began to confuse him. He was no longer sure just where the animal was. He turned his head in all directions trying to detect a movement. He was trapped, capable of being attacked from any side. An animal as quick as a cougar could be on him before he had opportunity to reposition his body and fire his gun. Even then, at best he'd get off one shot from an awkward angle. Maybe, he should just turn his horse around and race away. But, a cougar could then attack from behind and leap at him with little effort.

Keith sucked in a deep breath.

Okay, man, this is it. I can't just stay here and let the animal control my every move. I'm the human. I need to take charge. I don't have time to fool around with some crazy animal. I need to go forward in the hope that I can find the twins. I didn't spend time learning survival skills so I could end up not knowing how to deal with a situation like this. It's time for me to step up and take action. I need to force this animal to make his move.

Keith made a best estimate as to where he thought the big cat was hiding. He spotted a fallen tree branch on the snowy ground and reached down from his horse. Keith was able to break off a solid piece of wood. He lifted it up and prepared to throw it into the brush where he suspected the cat was. He held his gun steady, pointing it in that same area and braced himself.

Well, here we go. He's either going to charge me or he'll run away. Now, we find out what his play will be. That's better than playing this cat and mouse game. Haha—he is a cat, but I'm definitely not a mouse. So, here we go.

Keith threw the piece of tree branch as hard as he could.

CHAPTER TEN

Oh, the Weather Outside is Frightful

[December 23]

Collin Harrelson did not leave the Newman property, even though his Search and Rescue team was no longer out in the woods. He stayed in his vehicle with the heat blasting where he could also maintain radio contact with Sheriff Holliday and Keith Hughes. In truth, his heart hurt too much for him to let go right now. He always took every search effort personally and hated to ever accept failure. But, losing two little five-year-old children? That was beyond acceptance.

Yes, he would bring his team back in the morning, but it would no longer be a rescue mission. They would be attempting to provide closure for the Newmans.

Jody rose from the bed, still crying, but more in control than she had been just a short while earlier. She stared outside and noticed the Sheriff's Department vehicle with someone still in it sitting there on the property. She needed to do something to help stabilize her mind, so she dressed herself warmly, went into the kitchen, got a cup of hot chocolate, and stepped outside to bring it to whomever was in that vehicle. As Collin saw Jody approaching, he leaned his body over towards the passenger door to help Jody get in.

"Thought maybe this might help a bit," Jody said. "Wasn't sure whether to bring hot coffee, wassail, or hot chocolate."

The aroma of hot chocolate filled the cab of the vehicle.

"Ah, thank you.This'll do just fine. It's Jody, right?" Collin said.

"Yes, I'm Jody. Anything new you can tell me?"

Harrelson could readily see from the puffiness and redness on her face that Jody had been crying a great deal.

"Jody, Sheriff Holliday was careful not to get into too much detail when he spoke to all of you. Lord knows, your family is going through an enormously difficult time."

Even now, Harrelson was careful with his words. He couldn't think of situations any more stressful than what the Newmans were dealing with now.

"Jody, we do have a lead. It's highly-questionable, but it's at least something. Before this, we had pretty much nothing to work with. We've got one of our very best men working on it. His name is Keith Hughes."

Jody gasped at the mention of Keith's name, but said nothing to Collin Harrelson.

"Keith's tracking down a man in an extremely remote area of the woods. We believe there's a hunting cabin out there somewhere."

Harrelson paused, reached over, and placed his hands on Jody's. As he gazed into her eyes, he could sense the fear and anxiety within her.

"We don't know anything for sure, but it's possible that this man has the children."

Jody reached out and grabbed Collin's forearm and tightened her grip.

"Are you saying they may have been abducted?" Jody said.

"We don't know enough to say one way or another, but be assured that we'll know everything soon. We've got Keith out there. He'll never quit until we get the answers we need."

Harrelson's words triggered a recollection in Jody's mind. "I promise you," Keith told Jody just a few hours earlier, "I won't quit searching until we've got Rusty and Rylie back home safe and sound."

Tears filled Jody's eyes.

"The sheriff is also headed out that way with a team that includes your dad and brother," Harrelson said.

Teardrops continued to roll down Jody's cheeks as she let go of Collin's arm, dropped her head, and gazed downward.

Harrelson reached over, lifted her chin, and smiled at her.

"Hey, young lady, I can't imagine what you and your family are going through right now, but this is a time when we all need to cling tightly to hope and faith and usher in a Christmas miracle. What'd you say we do that together, huh?"

Jody's smile was tight, but it was real. A Christmas miracle—the very words that Keith uttered before he headed out into the forest. These people—people like Collin Harrelson and his wife, Rita, who was inside the cabin even now—people like the sheriff, the incredible number of neighbors who, in addition to the law enforcement personnel and first-responders, all showed up at a moment's notice today, people like Keith Hughes who was still out there somewhere in a remote area in a dark, freezing, formidable forest—these people had something Jody was lacking in. They possessed a value system that she no longer had. They had genuineness and a much better comprehension of what it means to be a neighbor and friend to others. She made more money than most of them and had the potential to make a whole lot more with her clothing line. But, they were all much wealthier than her.

Keith waited for the wind to temporarily subside before he threw the tree branch. He heard two sounds almost concurrently. The first was the sound of the branch landing in the brush. The second was the sound of an animal scampering away. Keith exhaled and relaxed his body a bit. For the moment, at least, his stalker had fled.

Keith continued to move forward, ever so slowly. Despite the scarf covering his face, ice crystals, with the aid of the winds, continued to slam against any opening to his skin, stinging him. To Keith, it was like being hit in the face with BBs or pellets from an air rifle. His visibility was limited to a foot or two and despite the fact that he was wearing safety goggles, he still found it difficult to fully open his eyelids. He reached for an oversized light windproof jacket he had at the back of the saddle and put it on over his clothes. Feeling numbness in his fingers and arms, he began to swirl his arms around in a circle like a windmill to increase blood flow to his hands and fingers.

Keith had expected he would have reached a cabin by now, but he saw nothing. He considered that he could be traveling in circles, despite his attempts to regulate his direction. His anxiety increased. Maybe, there wasn't a remote hunting cabin out here. He would feel a whole lot more confident if he at least knew that he was searching for something that definitely existed. Keith was tired, a bit disoriented, and discouraged, but he would not quit. No matter what, he was going to see this thing through. Of course, Keith had not taken the time to consider that he had now placed his own life in jeopardy. Without a heated structure in the area to replenish heat to his body, he would have difficulty, if it was at all possible, ever making it back to the Newman's home.

The horse moved slowly forward. Keith's mind began to drift. Jody had been gone for years and it was clear that Keith was no longer a factor in her life. But, over the years, Keith stopped by the Newman cabin from time-to-time when he was in that area. Jolene Newman was always warm and friendly to him. He knew the little twins. Picturing them in his mind now generated a sharp pain in his chest. He made a concerted effort to break away from those thoughts. He lifted his head and looked all around through squinted eyes. Nothing—no sign of a cabin, everything looked the same—cold, white, icy, and uninviting.

Another fifteen minutes passed when it happened. His senses burst into life. Even before he saw the old structure, he smelled smoke, wood smoke, expelled out into the area. As he drew nearer, he spotted a light coming from inside a wooden cabin. This was it! This had to be Caleb Banks' old hunting cabin. Keith could see that the cabin was once a state-of-the-art hunting place. Banks had money back then and he had the place well-built. It was worn after so many years of standing alone in what was a rough winter climate, but it still stood solidly on its own. An old Jeep sat at the side of the cabin.

Keith stopped, dismounted, and tied up his horse. As he neared the cabin, hoping he might be able to peer through a window, his foot turned up something in the snow that caused Keith to gasp. For hours Keith had been searching for a clue, some evidence of where the twins might be. Now, his breath stopped abruptly and his muscles tensed. He stared at a child's boot, most likely that of a little boy. Despite the snow and ice that covered it, Keith could see that the boot had not been on the ground very long. It could easily have been dropped there today.

Keith felt a chill racing up and down his spine. Little Rusty Newman—this had to be his boot. Rusty was either here or had been at this location.

Keith moved carefully towards the front porch and one of the windows. He could see the man inside the cabin with a knife in his hands bending down towards someone or something, but he was unable to discern for certain that Rusty and Rylie were in there. Then, the man turned away from what he was doing and walked over to check something he had boiling in a black kettle over the fire in the fireplace.

Keith's body was shaking and his hands were trembling. Even though the howling wind made it unlikely that anyone in the cabin would hear him, Keith moved farther away. He pulled out his gun and held it tightly in his left hand and held the radio with his right. He then called into Sheriff Holliday.

"Hughes calling Sheriff Roy. This is Hughes. Come in Sheriff."

The response was faint, accompanied by crackling and hissing sounds.

"Holliday here. Go ahead, Keith. Are you okay?"

"That's a roger, sir. Sheriff, I'm at the cabin. There's a man inside. Found a child's boot outside the place that could fit a five-year-old. I've been unable to determine whether the children are actually in there."

Hughes provided some rough coordinates for his location.

"It's real slow going for us in this weather," Holliday said. "We've got to be about a mile or so from you. Wait for backup, Keith. Do not enter the cabin."

Holliday knew he was facing a difficult decision. They had to assume that the man in there was Caleb Banks. The man had killed and then spent years in prison. There was no telling what his mental condition might be. If Keith did something that spurred a negative reaction in Banks, the man could kill the children, if they were alive and in the cabin, before Keith could stop him. Then again, Rusty and Rylie might already be dead or not even in that cabin.

At the same time, Keith Hughes was excellent with a gun and all forms of close physical contact. Surely, he could move deftly enough to subdue an older man. But, Keith had to be freezing from his extended exposure to the cold. His reflexes would be greatly hampered.

A myriad of thoughts raced through Sheriff Holliday's mind to a point where he was experiencing a mental overload. He bent over in his saddle and took several deep breaths in a concerted effort to calm himself.

Hughes broke the sheriff's thoughts.

"I can see the man's shadow through the window. He's got a raised knife again in his hand. Sorry, Sheriff Roy but I've got to act now. I can't wait. I'm going in, sir."

CHAPTER ELEVEN

Silent Night

[December 23]

Jody was back in her bedroom. She reached for her phone and prepared to send a text to FIMA's CEO, Alfred Monmouth. She quickly dismissed any question about where he might be and what he might be doing.

Why, he'll be working, of course. What else would he be doing? Work, business, success—these constitute the very essence of life itself. Nothing else really matters to a man like Alfred. And when you make money, you put yourself in position, as quickly as possible, to make more.

Well, it's time for me to tell him that I will not be at the office on Christmas morning. I could explain what's going on with my little brother and sister, but I honestly don't believe that would change anything. His response would likely be "Sorry, but there's nothing you can do about that now anyway and we'll pay for you to fly back. You can take some extra time away, if you'd like." But, no matter what, he'd expect me to be there in New York on Christmas morning.

Wait, hold on. This is wrong. I don't need to be focusing on Alfred. I don't need to try and blame everything on him. He's not the problem. I am. I lost sight of so much—my family, friends, neighbors, being there for others, and, even, the true meaning and value of Christmas, itself. I did that on my own and I started moving in that direction before I ever met Alfred Monmouth. I did this to myself.

Jody's fingers moved rapidly as she typed and sent the text informing Monmouth that she would not be there on Christmas Day. His response was immediate.

What? Perhaps, you do not understand, Jody, so let me make myself clear. Your attendance at this meeting is not optional. It is mandatory. There is no alternative to that, especially if you wish to retain your position at FIMA. I will expect your presence per our initial communications and agreement—AMon

No surprise. This was pretty much what she expected. In all fairness, she never told Alfred about the tragedy that she and her family were going through. Alfred Monmouth knew that she was with her family in Wyoming because she texted him from the airport before she left. There was no need to be unduly harsh with the man. The meeting Christmas morning and his reaction to her latest text were not the issues at play. She had to make changes in her life and she had to make them now. No one could do this for her.

In her next text, Jody formally resigned from her position with FIMA.

❧

Hughes moved carefully towards the cabin door. With his gun drawn, he checked to see if the cabin was locked. It was not. He would have to quickly open the door and be in the cabin before Banks had time to do much of anything. He did not want to provide Banks with any opportunity to react. Hughes started to make his move several times and backed down. Perspiration formed on his brow and at the top of his lips. His throat was dry and his hands within his leather gloves were clammy. He took in a deep breath.

Okay, Hughes. No time to back down now, bubba. You need to get inside this place and find out if the little ones are here. Remember, you have no idea if this guy is Banks and, if so, what he's up to.

Okay, okay, the first thing I need to know is whether Rusty and Rylie Newman are here in this cabin. If they are, I need to know if they're alive. If the children aren't in here, then my search continues. I still need to find out where they are.

One more deep breath and Keith Hughes made his move, thrusting open the cabin door. It opened towards the inside of the cabin ushering in blasts of cold air, along with snow and ice crystals. Banks was standing, cutting strips of cloth out of a sheet. He was initially startled to see Keith standing there with a gun pointed directly at him.

"Sheriff's Department, don't move," Hughes shouted. "Drop your weapon now. Put your hands on top of your head and don't make any moves or I'll drop you right where you stand."

Keith fought hard to keep his hand from shaking when he spotted what he did. They were there! Rusty and Rylie were lying together on the bed Banks had in the cabin. They were covered in blankets, clothes, pretty much whatever the man had available. An old black wood-burning stove was stoked as high as possible and spewing out heat. A fireplace at the back of the cabin had a blazing fire.

Banks dropped his knife on the floor. Then, following his initial reaction, Banks' demeanor radically changed. His face reddened. His jaw was clenched tight and his hands were curled up into fists. He glared at Hughes and began to scream. The man was in a frenzy now. He screamed so loud that Keith was surprised that Rusty and Rylie did not respond. Spittle flew from Banks' mouth as he continued to shout in a rage.

Jody stepped out into the main area of the family cabin. None of the women who had been sitting with her mom had left and none looked as if they wanted to leave. To these women, a neighbor had been unexpectedly thrust into a horrific situation. They felt and understood Jolene's pain and they intended to do all they could to somehow be there for her.

The women were joining in telling stories now, working hard to keep Jolene both calm and distracted. It appeared to be working to at least some degree. Jody was amazed at the strength in her mom. She knew her mother had to be aching inside, but, at the moment, Jolene Newman was speaking calmly with the other women and was not weeping.

Misty was alone in a corner of the room near the fireplace quietly picking at her guitar. Nick often said, "Some people read, others do crossword puzzles or Sudoku. Misty picks and strums."

Jody sat down next to her sister and put her arm around her. Misty leaned her head against Jody.

"How're you holding up?"Jody whispered in Misty's ear.

Misty never said a word, but the tears that began to roll down the cheeks of her face carried their own message.

Jody gently rocked her sister. Her mind was replete with a myriad of thoughts.

I haven't been here for Misty. I've been much too busy for her. She always looked up to me. In recent years, I've had little or no contact with her. Heck, let's be honest. I haven't been here for anyone in my family. My own heart is breaking for a baby brother and sister that I hadn't even seen in years. If it hadn't been for mama sending pics to me, I wouldn't have even known what Rusty and Rylie look like.

She held Misty tightly and continued to rock her and whisper softly to her. Jody glanced around the room. Women continued to feed the fire in the fireplace and serve hot drinks and pastries to each other. The Christmas decorations were vivid. At some point during the night, Jolene had someone turn the tree lights on. There was no doubt that the chatting throughout the room was more subdued than it normally would be, but, it was, by no means, somber and lacking in hope. Jody watched as one of the woman quietly approached her mom and Jolene nodded her head, turned towards Madelyn Stoner and smiled. Madelyn was a woman of substance. She and her husband, LeWand, owned one of the nearby dude ranches. Her clothes, her general appearance sent out a message that she was a wealthy woman, but here, in this setting, Madelyn was simply "one of the girls."

Following Jolene's acknowledging smile, Madelyn began singing *Silent Night*. Most every woman in the room shed tears, though none openly wept. Madelyn's voice was penetrating—just enough *vibrato* to produce a stronger or richer tone without generating a completely operatic sound.

After several verses, with Madelyn's urging, the other woman all joined in.

When Misty began to sing along with the others, Jody stared at her and the other women. Tears poured from Jody's eyes. She was witnessing another one of those otherwise intangible things that cannot easily be measured in dollars and cents—that thing otherwise known as *faith*.

"This is Sheriff Holliday calling Deputy Hughes. Keith, can you hear me? Keith, come in. This is Sheriff Roy calling Keith Hughes. Come in, Keith."

Collin Harrelson began rocking in his seat. His heart palpitations were strong. He could hear Roy Holliday calling in to Keith Hughes. Collin also was aware that Keith was not responding. Just moments earlier, Hughes communicated that he was going to enter the isolated cabin thought to belong to convicted felon Caleb Banks. Now, Keith was not answering the sheriff.

As he sat alone in his vehicle, Harrelson felt sick in the pit of his stomach. Out in a black frozen forest, Sheriff Roy Holliday felt the same.

CHAPTER TWELVE

I'll Have a Blue Christmas

[December 23]

Keith stood at the door with his gun still pointed at Banks. He didn't know what to make of the situation. Banks acted as if a man standing at the door with a loaded gun meant nothing to him. At the moment, there were things of much greater concern. He continued to scream in a rage. It appeared as if Banks, not Keith, was the person in control.

"Close that door. Close it now. What're you crazy?" Banks screamed. "Are you out of your mind? Don't let that cold air in here. These little ones can't take any additional cold temperatures. Listen, hot shot, you can do whatever you please with that gun of yours but do it in a heated cabin. You want to put a bullet in my head? Go right ahead. Have at it. But first, you need to… close… that… door."

Keith turned quickly and pushed the door shut. His eyes searched the room taking in everything he could, discerning all that was occurring. He saw the black Franklin Stove that was used to cook and warm up the place. At the far side from where Keith stood, there was the wood burning fireplace. There was a well on the property because a well pump was situated over a large metal sink. The area to the right of the door was the sleeping area where the bed was located that currently contained both Rusty and Rylie. To the left of the door where the sink was located, there was a small kitchen table, two chairs, and an old piece of furniture that appeared to contain kitchen items— plates, cups, small bowls, silverware, and more. Coleman lanterns and few scattered kerosene lamps provided the light throughout the room.

As he focused back on what Caleb was doing near the children, Keith's mouth fell open and he began to shake his head. His world was turned completely around at the realization that Caleb Banks was not a threat to Rusty and Rylie. Rather, the man was doing everything in his power to save their lives. He had rigged up some type of metal conduit that extended from the stove area and conveyed additional warm air or heat to the location where the children were. He had them covered with blankets, articles of his clothing, and whatever else he could use to keep them warm. He had any wet items of their clothing hanging to dry near the fireplace.

Banks was calmer now. He was still holding the sheet he'd been cutting strips from. He stared into Keith's eyes.

"I need to continue cutting up strips off that sheet. It's the closest I'm gonna come to gauze pads, hand towels, rags, whatever else I need here in this place."

Keith holstered his gun, nodded, and gestured to Banks that he was free to pick his knife up from the cabin floor. Banks returned to the task of cutting sheets.

Keith continued to stare at Rusty and Rylie as they appeared to be either asleep or unconscious lying still in the bed.

"Hey, Doc," Keith said. "How bad off are they? Are they going to make it? Will they live?"

Banks realized that this stranger knew his identity but said nothing about that.

"Under these circumstances, I don't know just what we're going to see. We're going to have to watch for the signs and indicators," Banks said.

He saw the puzzled look on Hughes' face and spoke again.

"Okay, let's begin with the fact that they were both unconscious when I brought them in here. Found them out there in the woods. They were cuddled together at the base of a tall pine tree. The girl was not breathing normally, so I administered CPR. As you can see, she's breathing normally now. That's a good sign.

Take a closer look at the children. You see they're both shivering right now? That's definitely a positive."

Keith furrowed his brow.

"How so, Doc?"

Banks went over and adjusted the blanket on Rylie.

"Because shivering is actually a process by which a body heats itself. When the core body temperature drops, the shivering reflex is triggered to maintain homeostasis. Skeletal muscles begin to shake in small movements, creating warmth by expending energy."

Banks turned again and adjusted Rusty's blankets, before turning back to face Hughes.

"And... uh... you can drop the doc label. They took my license away more than twenty years ago. Caleb will do."

"I'm Keith. Keith Hughes. The children are Rusty and Rylie Newman."

Banks pointed to the radio that Keith was holding.

"Can you use that thing to reach somebody?" Banks said. "These little ones are going to need something more than me and whatever I have available out here in this remote section of the woods. When I found them, they were in no condition for me to even try to bring them to a hospital."

Keith tried to reach the sheriff, Collin, anyone, but was unsuccessful.

"We've got Sheriff Holliday and a small team headed our way even now," Keith said. "The sheriff was gonna try and bring along an EMT with him, if possible. So, tell me, are we dealing with severe frostbite on these little guys?"

"More than," Banks said. "They're frostbitten, but we're also dealing with hypothermia. The shivering I referred to a few minutes ago, indicates their body temperatures are at least eighty-eight degrees. At eighty-three, the heart begins to beat irregularly. Drop another three degrees or so from there and it could be fatal. We've got to do whatever we can to keep their body temperatures from dropping and get them up higher."

Keith's composure changed. He stood rigidly, pinching the skin at his throat, and biting his lip. A surge of fear raced through his body.

"How bad off are they? Are they gonna be okay? How can I help?"

"We've got to warm up their bodies," Banks said. "You can help keep an eye on the things boiling on the stove, as well as making sure we have enough wood in the stove and logs in the fireplace. Those are the only sources of heat we have, plus blankets and body heat. For that reason, you need to keep yourself warm. You'll see that I have coffee brewed. I have the makings for hot chocolate and tea, and I already prepared some chicken broth."

Keith nodded.

"How can we tell if their body temperatures are improving?" Keith said.

"I wish we had a thermometer, but we don't," Banks said. "So, like I said, we look for signs. Increased movement, improved skin tone, and, hopefully, getting them conscious again where we can get some warm beverages in them. Our goal is to restore normal body temperature in them slowly — it's got to be slowly, son. Warming the body too quickly can cause shock and serious heart arrhythmias."

"Gotcha. So, what would be the next best thing we're waiting for now, Caleb?"

Banks hesitated. He was moving a kettle of hot water to a slightly cooler location on the stove. He turned back towards Keith. The look on Banks' face denoted a sense of hopelessness. He had taken all the steps he could on behalf of these two children and they appeared to be stabilizing. But, there was nothing additional that he could do — nothing to assure their conditions would improve and not regress.

"I stopped believing in miracles many years ago," Banks said, "but, right now, when it comes to these two little ones, I'm willing to start believing again."

Keith was silent. He had helped to find the twins and they were alive. But, there was no guarantee that they had been rescued in time.

Banks went over to the stove and poured two cups of coffee. He handed one to Keith.

"Now comes the hardest part," Caleb said. "Now, we wait."

Keith took a sip of his coffee. The two men were seated with an eye on Rusty and Rylie.

"A short while ago, you said that your medical license had been taken away. Did I hear that correctly?" Keith said.

Banks sat without saying a word. His head was down and when he lifted it, he stared off seemingly not focused on anything in particular. When he started to speak, he began with his eyes still not focused on Keith. He spoke in a monotone.

"I built this here cabin years ago as a place to stay when I came into the area to hunt. I was married while I was in med school, but my wife decided it was too much being married to a guy who had his head in a book all the time. We had no children when we divorced."

Banks lifted his head and made eye contact with Keith.

"You know who I am, so you are also aware that I served time. After I was released from prison, I came back here to live."

Keith took another sip of coffee before responding. He took turns wrapping each hand around the hot mug to help warm them.

"I only have a limited sketch of who you are, sir," Keith said. "Not much more."

"Served twelve of my twenty-year-sentence before they set me free," Banks said. Caleb stood up, lifted the coffee pot from the stove and added hot coffee to Keith's cup and his own, then sat down again.

"It all started with Marie, a young patient of mine. Marie lost her parents and a younger brother and sister in a house fire and suffered severe burns herself. As a fire victim, she was marred with scars. I was her primary physician through the years when Marie continued to receive skin grafts and undergo a slew of surgeries. Over the course of time, I took to loving her as the daughter I never had. I helped put her through college, where she met her husband, Paul."

Keith was listening intently. Every so often between statements, Caleb would sigh, as if he was releasing a great burden he carried within himself.

"I did not deliver babies in my practice, but I did have dinner with Paul and Marie a few times during her pregnancy."

Now, for the first time, Banks chuckled as his face lit up with a smile.

"Marie was radiant and I reveled in the joy that she and Paul had in anticipation of their first child. I tell you, I felt like an expectant grandfather the whole time."

Banks placed his coffee cup down and stared at his empty hands.His speech was much more hesitant.

"Malpractice by an obstetrician who was addicted to opiates, ended up in the deaths of Marie and her unborn child..."

Keith did a double-take as he listened to Banks' story unfold.

"I was devastated and had been drinking when I went to that doctor's office. Should have never gone there. We ended up in a heated argument that escalated into a fight. He grabbed my neck. I reached over on his desk, took a paperweight, struck him and ended up killing him. I claimed self-defense, but was convicted of second-degree murder. The victim was the son of one of the wealthiest men in the state and a top contributor to the political party associated with the judge, the governor, state attorney general, the majority of state senators, state reps, and more. The judge handed down a twenty-year sentence."

At his last hearing, Banks was almost not granted parole because he never expressed remorse for his crime.

CHAPTER THIRTEEN

Do You Hear What I hear?

[December 23]

The snow was still falling, but not as heavily. The blustering winds had subsided. It appeared as if the worst of nature's thrust was over. The storm left a healthy fourteen-inch layer of snow on the ground and drifts several feet high.

Sheriff Roy Holliday and his team had not yet spotted the cabin when he gathered everyone in a circle and spoke with them. He had to shout to be heard.

"Don't know how far away we are from the cabin. If Keith hadn't said that he found it, I'd be ready to believe it didn't exist."

The sheriff paused for a moment before continuing to speak. He wanted to choose his words carefully in order to assure that the men were on full alert, but not too spooked to function properly.

"Ain't been able to communicate with Keith since he reached the cabin and said he was going in," Holliday began. "I'm hoping, with the storm subsiding, we might get some better communicatin' now."

"Do you think Keith's in trouble?" one of the men asked.

"Can't say one way or another, but, at the same time, I ain't been able to get through to Collin, neither. Plus, Hughes is very capable of handling himself.

Listen. No matter what, we've got to be on full alert. I need the deputies in front as we first approach the cabin. Forrest, Nick, Danny, y'all need to stay back a bit until we've cleared the area and determined it's safe to enter."

"Hey, Roy," one of the deputies called out, "you think we gonna find the children there?"

"Well, like I told ya Keith said he found a little boy's boot in the area of the cabin. You know, we got Christmas coming on us real fast. I, for one, am lookin' for more'n toys from Santa Claus this year. What we need is some of that Christmas magic right about now."

All the men nodded their heads and offered words of agreement.

"What about this Caleb Banks?" another deputy asked.

Holliday shrugged and shook his head.

"We just don't know. There's no tellin' what so many years of prison does to a man. Until we know, we need to treat him as if he could be a dangerous man. That means we need to approach… "

"Hughes calling Sheriff Roy. Sheriff Roy, do you read me? This is Keith."

The voice transmitted over the radio startled everyone in the group. No one moved as they awaited news from Keith.

↔

Released from prison eight years ago at sixty-two-years-old, Caleb Banks had no family to turn to. He made a decision that he would go back to the old cabin that he still owned. He hadn't seen the place in close to fifteen years before he entered prison. But when he had it built, he spent extra money making it sturdy and able to withstand the extreme winter temperatures. In the past eight years, he'd already done a great deal to clean things up and make the place habitable once again. Caleb didn't need fancy or even comfortable. He just needed food and drink, protection from the elements, and the ability to heat the place up during the cold winter months. He also needed seclusion or isolation.

As Caleb Banks wandered the dark woods at night, he had ample time to think and reflect. Perhaps, this was where he belonged all along. Was that when he made his first mistake? Could it be that once he stepped out of his element, it served to curse his very existence?

Well, one thing he knew for sure now was that if he was going to survive the remaining years of his life, he would have to fend for himself. He had no one else in his life whom he could turn to or depend upon. He also had no one to blame for that, but himself. Of course, no one on earth would ever understand why he did what he did. How could they? He didn't understand it himself.

In one moment of disgust and anger, he changed the pattern of his life and future forever, leaving behind no one sympathetic to him and to what he had done. He was alone in that. But, what did that matter anyway? Having someone's sympathy was of no practical value anyway. It did not have the power to change the course of action his life took or get back so many lost years.

One advantage that he had was that he was not a stranger to the wilderness. Even those who knew him before he left this area had no idea just how strong his survival skills were. They were a meaningful part of his early life. He developed them as an escape from his shattered childhood. They helped him survive life with a drunken abusive father. The darkness he'd encounter when he'd slip out alone into the black woods at night was brighter than everything that existed within his childhood home. He had risen far above his early, somewhat primitive, years. Now it seemed as if he was intelligent enough to climb to the top, but not poised enough to remain there. He was supposed to be someone who saved lives, not someone who took life from others.

No longer confined within the walls of a prison or the steel bars of a cell, Caleb Banks was, nevertheless, still fettered by invisible chains. He was fated to live and die alone for whatever remaining time he had. He would live never caring again about the welfare of others. In truth, until now, until he encountered these two little ones unconscious in the woods, he assumed that any opportunity to be in position to care for someone else was no longer in play for him.

✍

"I'm... the cabin... Rusty... Rylie... here... I repeat... twins... here in... cabin... are alive."

Even though the storm had subsided a bit, Keith's transmission was scratchy, difficult to hear, and kept breaking in and out.

"Where is Caleb Banks, Keith?" Sheriff Roy asked. But, Keith did not answer. Once again, they lost radio contact.

Holliday called the men closer into a circle and shouted out to them.

"Keith Hughes says the twins are alive," the sheriff shouted.

The men with Holliday all broke out in loud cheering, drowning out whatever else the sheriff was starting to say. Forrest Newman and Nick were in tears as some of the others pulled their horses closer to them and exchanged high-fives, handshakes, and even a few hugs. The sheriff was attempting to quiet the group, then realized that the news was simply too great for people not to react. Within a minute or so, he did have a semblance of order and spoke again.

"I'll keep trying to get in touch with Keith to be sure we know exactly how to reach the cabin where he is with the children. I don't know yet where Caleb Banks is. We need to... "

"Keith Hughes calling Sheriff Roy. This is Hughes."

Silence ensued as Keith's voice interrupted the sheriff.

"Go ahead Keith."

"Sheriff... remote... back entrance to this cabin. Old road... barely noticeable off of Bear Springs Trail. Can be used for four-wheel drive emergency vehicles, ambulances... for the little ones..."

Once again, they lost contact with Keith. Sheriff Holliday was able to reach Connor Harrelson and transmitted the latest info to him.

"We'll track down that backroad Keith spoke about and get some emergency vehicles on the way," Connor said. When he disconnected and prepared to make the calls to send others out that way, Harrelson had to pause a moment because he was choked up and tears were filling his eyes.

Now, as Sheriff Roy and the others proceeded forward towards the cabin, their mood was considerably different than it had been earlier. They chatted with each other from their horses and even joked a bit. Their hearts were lighter. There was still much they did not know, but the news that the twins had been found alive was paramount.

Ned Wilkinson, who went back out into the woods with Holliday's team, bellowed out in his deep voice, "Merry Christmas, everyone. Merry Christmas."

✐

Banks was bending over tending to Rusty. He quickly turned around and spoke to Keith.

"Do you hear that, Deputy? The boy's breathing pattern has changed. Looks like we might be getting the beginning of that Christmas miracle I was talking about."

Keith ran over towards Caleb and Rusty in time to see the child open his eyes. Banks reached down and gently rubbed Rusty's face. He also made sure that Rusty was still adequately covered with the blankets.

"Well, hi there, young man. Now, don't you be afraid. You don't know me, but I'm a friend. And your daddy and brother will be here real soon," Banks said.

Rusty did begin to cry, but then he dozed off again. Rylie soon opened her eyes, as Rusty continued to come in and out of his stupor. Keith spoke softly to the two children, as Caleb Banks stood and headed for the stove. Before he reached the stove, he lifted both arms in the air, jumped up, and clapped his hands.

Chapter Fourteen

Have a Holly Jolly Christmas

[December 23]

Despite being in a groggy state, the twins were soon lucid enough to drink something warm.

"Caffeine is not good for hypothermia," Banks said, as he stirred the contents of two cups and handed one to Keith. This is warm chicken broth. I prepared it earlier for a moment just like this. He reached over and took the cup back from Keith. You've got to sit her up and use the teaspoon to feed her slowly."

Banks also propped Rusty up and began feeding him.

"There you go, little guy. That's good. Just a little at a time right now. Yeah, you're doing great. You finish this, I'll get you some more."

Rusty spoke for the first time. His voice was strained and a bit slurred.

"Are we… we out… someplace hidden?"

"Yes," Banks said. "This is an old hunting cabin. I used to stay out here when I was hunting instead of having to go back home each night. We just had to get you and your sister out of the cold for now until you could get back home."

Rusty's eyes opened wider.

"You got bears and stuff out here?"

Banks laughed as he stared at the little boy who was barely out of his groggy state and already exercising his imagination.

"Yeah, but you know Deputy Hughes, I believe. Well, he's a specially-trained bear killer and those bears know it. That's why we don't ever have a bear within miles of this cabin when Deputy Hughes is around."

"I'm cold," Rylie said—her first words since she opened her eyes. Keith spotted another blanket nearby and looked at Banks for approval. Caleb nodded. Keith placed it on top of Rylie with the other blankets and items of clothing that covered her.

Then, Caleb Banks, a convicted felon, and Keith Hughes, a deputy sheriff, fist-bumped each other, nodded their heads, and smiled.

"In all my years," Banks said, "this is the best Christmas ever. I never dreamed that I'd ever get another opportunity to do good for somebody again."

When Sheriff Holliday and the team arrived, the sheriff and two deputies entered the cabin with their guns drawn. Keith stepped directly in front of Caleb Banks. He smiled.

"Hey, Doc, it looks like our Christmas guests are all here now." The two men laughed. "Come in and close that door as quickly as possible."

Sheriff Holliday quickly grasped the situation.

"Well, if this don't beat all," the sheriff muttered as he holstered his gun and signaled to his deputies to do the same.

Rusty and Rylie were more conscious, but still in a weakened state. When they saw their daddy and Nick, they both cried. Forrest and Nick, per Banks' instructions, gently hugged them and smothered them with light kisses.

"Be careful not to rub their bodies," Caleb said.

Forrest and Nick both made a concerted effort to not let the children see them crying. Forrest later said that words could never describe what he felt when he first spotted the twins alive. He wasn't quite sure what to say when Rusty first spoke.

"Keith knows how to kill bears, Daddy. That's why we don't have none around."

Everyone chuckled, but Caleb and Keith laughed the hardest.

Caleb Banks greeted Sheriff Holliday. The sheriff stared at the man he had expressed a lack of trust towards.

"I... uh... I want to thank you for what you've done on behalf of these children," Holliday said.

Banks shrugged.

"Just doing what any man would or should do in a situation like this," Banks said.

Then, he pointed towards the stove and the kitchen area.

"Sheriff, you and your men are welcome to whatever you'd like. I've got coffee, hot chocolate, tea, and some coffee cakes and bread."

Banks used the sheriff's radio to speak with Harrelson and provide more detailed directions to the cabin. Over the course of time, the roads leading into the cabin had been all but eliminated by the weather and non-use. Caleb provided added insight to markers he placed on trees and bushes that will help the emergency vehicle drivers find their way in.

Then, Banks joined together with Danny Clark. The two men began to carefully examine the children. Danny had thermometers and other equipment to aid in taking vitals, such as body temperatures and blood pressure. Danny had chemical hot packs that were activated by squeezing the package. As Keith came over to assist, Caleb spoke to him.

"Place the hot pack on a neck, chest, or groin. Do not place one of these on an arm or leg. That could push cold back to the heart or lungs and cause their body temperatures to drop again," Caleb said.

Danny also brought gauze and several other first-aid items that were beneficial until the ambulances arrived.

"Well, sir," Danny said, "looks like you had everything covered. These children are looking good. Considering what their bodies went through, it's remarkable to see the shape they're in. Thank God it was you they ended up with."

Caleb later commented that the words spoken by Danny Clark were the most sublime words anyone had spoken to him in his entire life.

Forrest Newman was in tears as he thanked and hugged Caleb Banks for saving the lives of his children. For more than twenty years, Caleb Banks was identified as a man who had disgraced himself and his profession. Instead of saving a life, he had taken one in anger. Tonight, two little children owed their lives to him. Tonight, even without a valid license to frame and display on a wall, he was Doctor Caleb Banks once again.

Danny Clark also took time to examine Keith Hughes. He noted that Banks had placed little strips of cloth between

Keith's toes and had taken other emergency first-aid steps to combat frostbite.

Sheriff Roy and his team were all jampacked into Banks' cabin, occasionally jostling and bumping into one another. But, they were elated to be out from the cold freezing temperatures. On this night, an old hunting cabin that had been dormant for years was alive again and providing warmth and shelter to a group of men and two little children who had escaped death.

One would think that being the person to enter a room filled with women to inform them that two little five-year-olds had been found and were alive would be the easiest task and most rewarding one to conduct. But, for Collin Harrelson, it was one of the most difficult and challenging things he ever had to do. Despite the fact that it was the best news he could ever bring to a mother and two sisters, along with a group of neighbors, Collin had to tell everyone without breaking down and sobbing as he spoke. That was the most difficult aspect of it. After all, he was not only a man, he was a lawman, a tough guy who openly carried a gun, arrested bad guys, and defended women and children. But, all Collin had to do was stop for just a moment and think about all that had occurred tonight, remember the hidden moments of despair when he feared they had been unsuccessful in saving the lives of two precious children, and his eyes filled with tears again.

Now, he was supposed to stand in front of a room filled with women, including the mother and sisters of Rusty and Rylie Newman, and bring them this news? He'd rather be in a dark alley with two huge thugs wielding clubs than attempt this.

When he stepped into the room, it was as if someone pulled a plug. Everyone stopped speaking. They focused upon Harrelson waiting for him to speak. It was so quiet, he was sure that they all could hear his stomach rumbling and making weird sounds.

He looked quickly at Jolene Newman, then spotted Jody and Misty. When he did, he felt as if his heart was laying out on the floor pulsing rapidly. There was no way he would ever focus on them again.

Harrelson was so choked up, he honestly doubted he would ever be able to finish a sentence. But, he never had to. Once he got out the words, "The children have been found and are safe," the room erupted. The women were cheering, leaping for joy, and crying so loud nothing else he would say could possibly have been heard. Jody hugged Misty tightly as they both sobbed. Then, they went and joined in a three-way hug with their mom. As they hugged, they all sobbed and were jumping up and down like lottery prize winners who just found out they'd hit the jackpot.

Everyone in the room moved around hugging one another, often more than once. There was not a dry eye to be found.

Reverend Watkins' wife, Miriam, was able to quell the celebration for a moment as she led the women in a prayer of thanks for this miracle of Christmas. Then, the women started celebrating again. In the midst of all the jubilation and the commotion it generated, Jody was able to slip away into her bedroom without being noticed. She walked over towards the bed, then fell upon it face-first and sobbed again. The bed was shaking. Her tears were soaking areas of the bed she would sleep in that night. She could not remember ever being so happy and so thankful in her life.

When Jody stepped back out into the main room, several of the woman were dancing together in a circle, while Misty strummed a fast-paced song on her guitar. Two of the women in the room took the bowls of popcorn and began to thrust kernels into the air like confetti. Jolene Newman was among the women laughing heartily at this gesture.

One of the women dancing on the floor grabbed Jody's hand and pulled her into the dance. Jody joined in and as she danced with these women she thought of what Alfred and her co-workers would think if they saw her acting like this. She wished they did.

West Park Hospital in Cody is the place where the ambulances brought Rusty, Rylie, and Keith Hughes. Danny Clark traveled with Keith. Forrest Newman and Nick were with the twins. Back at the Newman home, Collin Harrelson gathered his wife, Rita, Jolene Newman, Jody, Misty, and Lana and headed to Cody.

During the trek to the Cody hospital, the twins were already chatting more. One day, Forrest would talk with the twins again and warn them never to run out into the woods again. But this would not be the day or time to do so.

On the drive to the hospital, Collin used the time with Jolene and the girls to fill them in on more of the details of what had occurred.

"Keith Hughes was amazing. He refused to quit. It was bitter cold, the night in the forest was black as coal, a threat of nightly predators existed. Based upon departmental safety protocol, all personnel were supposed to be recalled.

But, Hughes asked, begged actually, for special permission from me and, ultimately, Sheriff Roy to press on. He spotted human footprints in a very remote area and believed that they could somehow help lead us to Rusty and Rylie. Sheriff Roy did some quick investigating and learned that a convicted felon once had a hunting cabin way out in that area—a medical doctor by the name of Caleb Banks, a convicted murderer.

Keith reached the cabin first, while Sheriff Roy and a team that included Forrest and Nick all headed that way. Ends up that Banks found the twins unconscious cuddled together at the base of a tree and carried them quite a distance to his cabin. They were suffering from hypothermia. Banks saved their lives."

Misty and Lana gasped and shed tears as they listened to Collin. Jody was stunned by all that she was hearing and making note of the various heroes who were key factors in saving the lives of her little brother and sister. Jolene smiled with an inner joy that none of the horrible things that might have occurred did and her babies were now safe from all harm.

Was there ever a more precious Christmas present that a mother could receive?

Chapter Fifteen

It's the Most Wonderful Time of the Year

[December 23-24]

It was a late night for everyone in the Newman family, but, it was ending so well, they were hardly aware of the lateness of the hour. The hospital doctors examined the twins, once again, and marveled at how well they were faring despite all they had endured.

"The first aid care administered to these children undoubtedly saved their lives," said Sam Caldwell, a retired surgeon and a current member of the West Park Hospital Board of Directors. Doctor Caldwell would normally not be in the ER, but when he heard that the Newman twins were being brought in, he left his home and drove to the hospital to await their arrival. When Danny Clark came by, Doctor Caldwell called to him.

"Are you the EMT responsible for the initial emergency care these two little ones received? You know, without that, it'd be a totally different story tonight when it comes to their lives and... "

"Pardon the interruption, Doc, but that credit doesn't belong to me. An older man, a former medical doctor, gets the credit there. He found the children unconscious in the forest, carried them a considerable distance to his cabin, and, using whatever makeshift tools and supplies available to him, did everything he could to save them."

"Remarkable," Caldwell said. "Simply remarkable."

❦

Keith Hughes was sitting up in his hospital bed when Jody entered the room. His feet and hands had already been soaked in warm water until they turned red and were wrapped in sterile dressings. The strips of material that Caleb had placed between Keith's toes were replaced with gauze prior to the feet being wrapped. A medicated salve had been applied to areas of his face that appeared to be chafed and raw.

The moment she saw him, tears filled Jody's eyes. She gently kissed his face.

"How can we ever thank you, Keith. After what you did for Rusty and Rylie, we'll always be indebted to you."

Keith smiled and gently shook his head.

"I was merely doing my job, Jody. What happened tonight is the very reason why I chose to join the Sheriff's Department. I wanted to help save lives, to be someone who makes a difference in the lives of others. That's why, in addition to my responsibilities as a deputy, I went through the additional training to be a member of the Search and Rescue Squad. Having the opportunity to help Rusty and Rylie is the greatest Christmas present I could ever receive."

Tears flowed freely from Jody's eyes. She gently reached out and took one of Keith's bandaged hands in hers.

"Hey, no real damage here at all," Keith said, believing Jody was crying at the sight of his bandaged hands and feet. "This is all precautionary stuff because I had some degree of frostbite. No big deal. Best I can tell, I still have ten fingers and ten toes," he said, followed by a chuckle.

Keith was unaware that despite her sensitivity to Keith's injuries suffered while going beyond the call of duty to find and save the twins, Jody was crying for reasons beyond all that. She wept at seeing the selflessness of this young man towards others. She cried at the very thought of what Keith endured alone out at night under freezing conditions. Jody's tears also flowed at the continued realization of just how blind she had become in recent years. She cried because she was ashamed. She cried tears of joy because she was now seeing clearly.

The doctors at the hospital were of the opinion that if things remained as they presently were, Rusty and Rylie would be able to return home after an overnight stay. They would continue to need monitored medical care while at home but being home on Christmas Eve Day and waking up Christmas morning with the family added to everyone's joy. Jolene would spend the night at the hospital with Rusty and Rylie.

The doctors also determined that Keith Hughes was in position to return home after spending this one night at the hospital. Keith lived alone in an apartment just outside of Cody, but the nurses would show him how to treat his injuries and replace bandages. In addition, he, as well as the twins, would have access to a home care health nurse.

Forrest and Jolene Newman asked Keith if he would be willing to come to their home for lunch on Christmas Day and Keith, after receiving their assurance he would not be intruding on their family time together, agreed to come.

A sheriff's deputy brought Forrest, Jody, Nick, Lana, and Misty back home. When they entered the cabin, it was spotless, having been cleaned by all the women before they left earlier that evening. Jody laughed as she recalled the women throwing popcorn in the air while celebrating that Rusty and Rylie had been rescued.

At the end of what was surely the most emotionally-draining day of their lives, Forrest, Jody, Nick, Lana, and Misty were all exhausted and, upon entering their bedrooms, fell asleep immediately.

Caleb Banks sat alone in his isolated cabin. What a night! He'd gone from a cabin overflowing with people, including two children he had rescued, back to the norm of being the only person around for miles. When he was discharged from prison, he expected he would be alone. He had no family, no friends, no one he could or would turn to. A man like him would be like a leper to decent folks in society. He understood that. The fault did not lie with others. This was his fate brought on by himself.

Before his impulsive rage changed the entire course of his life, Banks reveled in every opportunity he had to help others. On this night, he experienced something that he thought he would never again have opportunity to do. He was involved in what proved to be a successful life-saving effort. It felt good—the only thing he felt good about in more than a decade.

∾

By late morning, Rusty and Rylie were back home utilizing wheelchairs that were provided through the hospital. Within a few hours, Jolene had them both down for a nap, which she, in the same room as the twins, also engaged in.

All the gifts were wrapped, the Christmas meal was planned, so other than the extra care needed for Rusty and Rylie, there was nothing major that Jolene had to do. Christmas would arrive on its own and she would be free to enjoy it with the others. And every time she thought of her two youngest children, her heart grew warm and a smile covered her face.

∾

Christmas Eve and, despite being alone, Caleb Banks was still basking in an inner joy from the fact that the Newman twins had been successfully rescued. In the evening shortly before the sun was preparing to settle in for the night, Caleb Banks had just loaded wood in the stove and placed logs on the fireplace grate when he thought he heard a thump on the front porch. He paused for a moment to listen again but did not hear anything further. He placed a pot of water on the stove when he heard the unmistakable sounds of music.

"Hark the herald angels sing, glory to the newborn king... "

Caleb ran to the cabin door and opened it. There were as many as thirty carolers. He did not know any of the women. Among the men, he recognized Sheriff Roy Holliday, Danny Clark, Forrest, and Nick Newman.

The porch was littered with gifts and items of food. Juicy succulent grapes were hanging from the porch bannister. He spotted a whole cooked ham, several breads, corn, and freshly-picked green beans and squash that had obviously been grown in local greenhouses. There were a few homemade pies, a cake, and cookies. He also spotted a few new blankets, two pillows, a man's robe, and slippers. Several coolers filled with ice and dry ice were provided so he would have an extended time for storage.

The carolers continued to sing. Caleb had tears in his eyes as he stood at the open cabin door feeling awkward over the fact that a group of people had come to honor him.

Following a song, Forrest Newman spoke.

"Merry Christmas, Caleb, from all of us and a good many others unable to be here tonight."

Caleb stood speechless with his mouth open.

"For some reason," Sheriff Holliday said, "we figured you probably don't get many carolers out this way, so we decided to drop by."

Everyone laughed, including Caleb Banks.

Caleb thanked everyone for the items left on his porch. Someone in the crowd asked why Santa came earlier out here in the forest, drawing a laugh from the group.

"Listen, I don't deserve all of these things from decent people who... "

It was the sheriff who interrupted Banks.

"Let's stop with all that talk about deserving and decent folks," Holliday said. "Even before you did what you did for the Newman twins, you have as much right as anyone to be given a second chance. You paid for what you did. Time for you to move on, Banks. And we're all willing to move on with you."

The group applauded at Sheriff Roy's comments, causing Banks to, once again, gather tears in his eyes. He had a real difficulty forgiving himself for what he had done. He didn't expect anyone else to be willing to do so.

"And as to your comment about receiving these things from decent people," Holliday said, "well, I'm included amongst them, so they can't be all that decent, you know?"

Everyone roared again with laughter.

"Now," the sheriff said, "let's get these things inside before we all freeze to death."

CHAPTER SIXTEEN

It's the Best Time of the Year

[December 25]

Sitting around the Christmas tree with a mug of hot coffee, while listening to the squeals of delight from little Rusty and Rylie, was yet another special moment for Jody. It wasn't the gifts—it wasn't the gifts at all. Rather, it was the joy that draped over everything that morning. And, in the case of Rusty and Rylie, the fact that they were even there and functional was the greatest thing of all.

The twins were simply too young to fully comprehend that they had been so close to not surviving the ordeal just two nights earlier. Every giggle and laugh served to deny everything that had occurred out in the black frozen woods. That was then, this was now. And the now was filled with joy and love.

In the past few years, there was no joyful opening of gifts on a Christmas morning for Jody. And, even though gift opening should not define Christmas in Jody's mind, it was far better than waking up at sometime around 2:00 p.m. with a hangover. Everything here was so innocent in a manner Jody had not experienced in years.

∽

Sheriff Roy got Caleb Banks to agree to come to Christmas lunch at the Holliday home. The sheriff's wife was pleased that her husband had opened his heart to a man he initially had strong suspicions about.

"Well, I'll tell you right now," Holliday told his wife, "this is one time when I'm glad that my initial thoughts about someone were wrong. I give a lot of credit to Keith for pushing on his hunch and pursuing the tracks he found. He got to Banks before we did and cleared up any questions we had about Doc Banks."

Banks had disappeared off the map and violated his parole over these past eight years. Holliday did not have authority over that, but he already was working on a strategy to make contact with people who could, indeed, help.

Caleb Banks proved to be a wonderful houseguest. Despite the fact that he was a convicted felon who spent more than a decade behind bars, it was apparent that the man was not defined by an isolated violent act. Banks was polite and an excellent conversationalist.

Following dinner, Sheriff Roy took Caleb aside to talk with him.

"Danny Clark will be stopping by for dessert," the sheriff told Banks. "Meanwhile, let's you and me have a little chat. I don't know if you have any interest at all, but I've done some checking. You lost your license to practice medicine, but, as best we can tell, you are not precluded from working in the medical field in some capacity. Doctor Ernest Caldwell is a retired surgeon who is actively on the hospital Board at West Park. He's been interested in setting up a small urgent care clinic out towards the area where the Newmans live. Caldwell was in the ER when the twins arrived yesterday. Forrest Newman helped the doc get a beautiful horse broken in time for a gift to one of his daughters on her graduation from high school. Doc was very appreciative for that and thinks highly of Forrest. When he heard the twins were coming in, he wanted to personally look in on things. He saw what you had done preliminarily for the children. He'd like to meet with you, Caleb."

Banks was stunned at the news.

"Caldwell said something about you taking some refresher courses which the hospital would pay for. Anyway, give this some thought and, if you're genuinely interested, we'll set you up to meet with Doctor Caldwell."

When Danny Clark showed up, he had an immediate rapport with Banks. In addition to what they shared with regard to medicine, Danny had been told about Caleb's renowned outdoorsman skills.

"We passed a trap that contained the remains of a deer. But, I've never seen a trap like that before," Danny said.

"Well, I'd been working on that for some time," Banks said. "I wanted a trap that'd hold an animal but not injure it. Allows a hunter to set free any animal that he or she was not hunting for. Also, for obvious reasons, I'm prohibited from carrying a gun and, if I set the trap up correctly, I could take out the animal humanely. For months now, I tried, but either caught nothing or the animal escaped. I finally had success and, just when I saw I had trapped a deer, I saw what looked like clothing on the ground at a nearby tree and ran over to investigate. That's when I found the Newman twins and knew I had to get them inside my cabin as quickly as possible. I was running away from the area carrying a child in each arm when I heard the rogue cougar in the area. He must have been nearby the entire time."

"Good thing you got the twins out of there when you did," Danny said.

"Way I see it," Sheriff Roy said, "be it the cold or the cougar, either way you saved the lives of those little ones."

Banks said nothing.

"What say you and me spend some time together one day and you show me how you built that trap?" Danny said.

Caleb laughed and agreed.

⁂

Following lunch at the Newman's, they all agreed to take a little break before having dessert. Jolene put the twins down for a nap, while Jody and Keith sat together on the fireplace hearth.

Jody took the time to redress Keith's bandages.

"Okay now. You tell me if I'm not doing this right," Jody said.

Keith smiled. "You're doing it perfectly, Jody. Just like a professional nurse."

"You know," Jody said, "you took a real chance being out there so long in the frigid weather, Keith. I'm so thankful that you didn't permanently injure yourself."

Keith stared into Jody's eyes. He spoke hesitantly, as if he was weighing his words and making a concerted effort to control his emotions.

"The thought of Rusty and Rylie somewhere out there... well, that was something I... couldn't live with. I had to find them, Jody. No matter what, I had to keep... trying."

Jody lifted her head from wrapping the gauze on Keith's hands and their eyes met again.

"When are you headed back?" Keith asked.

Jody paused, dropped her head, and did not answer right away. Then, she turned her head towards Keith.

"I-I honestly don't know right now. I had a flight scheduled but canceled it."

She did not mention that the flight would have been on Christmas Eve Day. She also did not mention that she had quit her job.

"I understand with all that occurred with Rusty and Rylie, you'd want to be sensitive to things before heading back," Keith said. "Surely your boss would understand under the circumstances."

"It's more than that, Keith. I mean, of course, my little brother and sister are at the top of my concerns, but there's a lot going on in my mind. Being back here has reminded me of so much that I've lost in recent years, so much that I've missed."

"Yeah, well, you were always so special. With your smarts and talents, there has never been any limits to how far you could succeed. I guess I knew that all along, but it took awhile before I was willing to accept that you were bigger than this place, bigger than a guy like me."

Tears began to gently roll down Jody's cheeks.

"Hey," Keith said. "What's wrong? Have I said something to offend you?"

Jody struggled to respond to Keith's questions. She spoke, even as she sobbed.

"N-no… y-you've… j-just s-spoken the t-truth. I threw everything away, Keith. I lost sight of my f-family, of things that really m-matter in life—like back when you used to love me."

Keith's body stiffened as he froze momentarily, then pulled Jody close and held her tightly in his arms. As he did, he whispered in her ear.

"No, Jody, there is no 'used to'—that never happened. That would be impossible."

"W-what, Keith? What?"

"That I could ever stop loving you. Never happened. Not even for a single day."

Crystal clear beads dropped from Jody's eyes and slid down her face. To Keith, they looked like exquisite pearls.

"I thought of you all the time," Keith said, "and saw you in my dreams, in everything around me. No, Jody, I never stopped loving you and no matter what you do from now into the future, I never will."

Jody leaned into Keith and welcomed his kiss. It was a deep kiss—a kiss filled with missed yesterdays and a lifetime of tomorrows. It was the kind of kiss that can only emanate from two hearts filled with true love.

Keith smiled and whispered in Jody's ear.

"Merry Christmas, my love. Welcome back."

The twins recovered fully. Misty continued to do well in school with plans to go to college to acquire a degree in music. Nick and Lana announced their engagement to be married and were already planning their wedding—simple, country, outdoors, beautiful—maybe even atop horses.

Sheriff Roy Holliday was unopposed in the fall election. With help from the governor and other key officials, Roy Holliday was able to assure that Banks would not be returned to prison for violating his parole. West Park Hospital hired Caleb Banks to run an urgent care clinic located between Cody and Powell. Jesse and Marilyn Castings, neighbors to the Newmans, had a mobile home situated on their property that their daughter and her husband occupied before acquiring their first home. Caleb rented the place.

On days off from time-to-time, Banks, Danny Clark, and Keith Hughes would head to Caleb's cabin and spend some time hunting, fishing, or just enjoying the outdoors. On a few occasions, Nick Newman joined them.

Jody accepted a professorship at her alma mater, Oregon State University, where she taught classes in fashion design and marketing. As a result, she was able to come home regularly and did so.

Jody, despite her resignation from FIMA, had retained her rights over the sportswear fashion line she had created. The line sold to a German company. Under her prior contract, she shared in the royalties with Fashions Imaginations, Inc. The sale generated a healthy income to her. She chose to begin putting the money away with the intent that it was something she and Keith would use after they were married and ready to acquire their first home. Keith was promoted to lieutenant and supplemented his income by teaching a survivor course. His reputation following the rescue of Rusty and Rylie was so strong, he had to teach two sessions in order to include all of the applicants.

Jody quickly learned to see and appreciate the beauty of things all around her—things not associated with profits or price tags. A morning sunrise, springtime flowers, sunlight peeking through the leaves of trees in the forest, leaves changing color in the fall, and a snowfall bathing everything in white all brought joy to her. She relished the times she spent with her family and with Keith.

And, as an integral part of the life changes she continually experienced, Jody learned to once again love and embrace Christmas—the time when, in her opinion, the hearts of people became the most beautiful.

The End

THANK YOU

Thank you so much for reading this book. Christmas has always had a special place in my heart, so writing a Christmas novella is particularly enjoyable for me.

Please, if you enjoyed this book, consider entering a positive review on Amazon. Even just a few words saying you enjoyed this will help a great deal.

Thank you.

And, please check out all of my writings at: www.vincentsachar.com.

www.ingramcontent.com/pod-product-compliance
Lightning Source LLC
Chambersburg PA
CBHW060636130626
46555CB00002B/834